FEAR

Short Stories
by
Chris Bullard

ISBN: 978-1-945917-11-0

Printed in the United States of America

Cover Design: Christopher Reilley
Author Photo: Janice Bullard

Also by Chris Bullard:

You Must Not Know Too Much (Plan B Press, 2009)
O Brilliant Kids (Big Table Publishing, 2011)
Back (CW Books, 2013)
Dear Leatherface (Kattywompus Press, 2014)
Grand Canyon (David Roberts Books, 2015)
Leviathan (Finishing Line Press, 2015)
High Pulp (Kattywompus Press, 2017)

"Making other books jealous since 2004"

Big Table Publishing Company
Boston, MA
www.bigtablepublishing.com

Acknowledgements

I thank Casey Tingle and Janice Bullard for their efforts in editing this manuscript.

Some of the stories in *Fear* appeared in the following journals:
"Marriage *à la Mode*" – *Blotterature*
"Drone" – *Nebula Rift*
"We've Only Just Begun" – *Perihelion*
"The Coat" – *The Sideshow*

For Josephine
with the hope that she will always be able to face her fears.

Table of Contents

The Sleeping Beauty

My wife, Shirley, died and it took a year of pain and misery. Lord, that woman suffered. She had stomach cancer and even the pills didn't help. I never saw anyone in such pain.

Anyway, after my wife died, my daughter Becky cried every night for her. She was only twelve that year and her mother had been everything to her. Me, I was around, but I was never a daddy that Oprah would have approved of. I loved her though.

I had been getting disability for a few years. It wasn't a lot of money, but it helped with the bills and when Shirley was working we made out all right. I guess you could say I had my own issues. I kept to myself. I didn't like being around other people. I thought Becky was like me, that she didn't need friends. I thought she could get by on her own.

So, it took me a while to respond and to realize what my wife's death had done to Becky. One night she came to me while I was lying on the sofa, watching TV. I always had the TV on, but I never really paid attention. I guess I was just lost in my own dreams.

She was bawling her poor little heart out. And then she lay down beside me while her hot little tears fell on my undershirt. I mean, I could feel my shirt really getting soaked. And I hugged her and tried real hard to think of what I could do to make her feel better. What I could do to ease the pain, so to speak.

I remembered some of the stories that my Mom had told me. You know, bedtime stories, but the real old ones, fairy tales, I mean Mom knew I loved those stories. I was the littlest one and sometimes my brothers would push me around. So, when I got real sad, she would tell me one of those stories.

One of my favorites was about Lazy Jack and how he'd done all these foolish things and how he'd been so ridiculous that he'd made the princess smile, even though she was the princess who would never smile. So, I told Becky that story and she listened and, God dammit, I could see a little smile on her face. Then, I tickled her and she said stop, but I knew she didn't want me to, so I kept making her laugh.

I let her go to sleep right there beside me. And I thought, maybe, for a minute or two, she's forgotten about her mother and the suffering we've all gone through.

She loved those stories. Hell, we both did. It was the fantasy that drew you in and made you forget everything else. I mean, there was always some task that the king would set a boy to. If you do this, the king would say, you'll win my daughter's hand and the keys to the kingdom. I guess it was sort of the lottery of olden days.

In the stories girls always had to venture out and deal with wolves and beasts. I told Becky, you see, those girls never got scared because they knew the beast would always turn out to be good and kind.

I would take Becky to the library and we'd check out something by Hans Christian Anderson or the Grimm brothers. Every night I'd read to her until she went to sleep. Maybe, I indulged her too much, but those stories made her so happy.

I got her one of those princess costumes from a catalogue. They have them for Halloween. Becky would put it on every night when I'd read her a story. And, okay, this really sounds crazy, but I got some cinder blocks from a construction site and I stacked them up in the cellar, and they made a wall that really looked like it was part of a castle.

I would come down the stairs and Becky would be on the other side of the basement behind the cinder blocks and she would call out to me, "What is your quest, good sir?" and I would call back, "To read the Princess a bedtime story, of course." Then, she'd say, "Enter," and pretend to lower the drawbridge for me.

Sometimes, I'd read a story and we'd make a game of it. I'd read about the boy who found a dish with a white snake on it and when he nibbled on the snake, he could understand what the animals were saying. Or, how the Princess poured a cauldron of fish over the boy who didn't know fear and how that taught him what it was like to be scared.

We had such good times. I mean, sure it would have been better if Becky could have found some friends, but we were living on the edge of North Philly in one of those neighborhoods that had gone bad real quick. All the girls her age were already shooting up and joining gangs, for God's sake. It was bad enough that she had to go to school with them.

This went on for about a year and then I ran into the wicked witch. She wasn't the Disney wicked witch, of course. She didn't have a big bucket, or a pointed hat. She was sort of squat with big glasses and curly hair and she wore a business suit. But she was the wicked witch, alright.

She was some sort of assistant principal at Becky's school. She phoned me one day and said I had to come in for a conference. I asked Becky what was going on, but she just shrugged and said, "I don't know," in that sweet little innocent voice. So I went. That's when the wicked witch unloaded all this crap about Becky and how she was saying inappropriate things to the boys and how she had inappropriate physical contact with one kid and how she wasn't acting appropriately for her age.

Appropriate was a big word for the wicked witch. It worked like a spell for her. She could make fathers disappear with that one. I wanted to start a big bonfire for the witch, but I only said "good day" and went home to wait for Becky. I knew the witch wanted to take Annabelle Lee away from her kingdom by the sea.

That night, I made her favorite, macaroni and cheese, and I served her a big glass of sparkling apple cider. She thought it was like having champagne. After dinner, I read her Sleeping Beauty. "What do you think it's like to sleep for a hundred years?" I asked her, but she was already asleep. The pills that the doctors had prescribed for her mother were pretty strong. I figured that I had put enough of them in her apple cider.

"A hundred years. That's all it takes until Prince Charming comes," I said. I had already taken the top off her toy chest and moved it down to the cellar. I took Becky and laid her in the toy chest. We had this glass table top that her mother had bought from Pier One and I put it on the top of the chest. It was like The Glass Coffin. You could see how peaceful she was there.

So, call me a knight errant or a boy with no fortune or God damn Puss-in-Boats, but I'm off to see the world and do great deeds. Maybe, I'll keep going for a hundred years and, one day, the stag will call to me or the fairy will give me a glass key, and I'll find her again and take her out of the coffin where she's been sleeping and give her a kiss.

The princess will wake up and someone will say, "They lived happily afterwards. The end." It'll be the best story ever.

Marriage *à la Mode*

Stem cells made everybody physically immortal, but didn't do anything about senility. Minds deteriorated over time. Every so often you had to get a new identity with a new set of memories. These identities were stored electronically and could be downloaded from the Cloud.

You couldn't ask to stay yourself because you'd be imprinting over the same brain cells that were giving you all the problems. You had to awaken new brain cells by accepting a donor personality. That's why I'm now Lester Potts, an accountant. The neuro-scientists are forbidden by law to tell me whom I used to be.

Anyway, my problem is that Lester still loves his wife and thinks about her all the time, wondering about what she is doing and thinking about how lovely she looks. My days are filled with thoughts of Lester's wife.

After some time suffering a painful, unrequited love for this woman I decided that I had no choice but to find her and attempt to rekindle the passion that had existed between these two people, one of whom I now was. Eventually, I uncovered the name of someone who had become Lester's wife through a personality transfer.

This woman was not the slender blonde Lester remembered, but, rather, a middle-aged brunette trying to wear dresses designed for women who were a size 4. Nevertheless, I approached her, hoping to renew our imprinted relationship, only to discover that her memories of Lester were more ambivalent than my own.

She had once loved Lester, but no more. Lester had done some terrible wrong to her and although I promised her that Lester could change and that the love of her implanted personality could be the force that would make my implanted personality a good man, she rejected my attempts at reconciliation.

That the woman whom Lester loved and whom I had been programmed to love would reject us was so devastating that it broke both our hearts.

I was left with no way to assuage the hunger I have for another man's wife, who hates him, but will have nothing to do with me because I am also that man. All I have is the comfort of being pals with other guys who have also undergone the treatment to become Lester Potts.

I always find them drinking at the same bar where Lester hung out. Did I mention that Lester drinks excessively? I recognize them by their look of perplexed despair.

When I meet such a fellow I have the opportunity to reminisce with him about our wife and the wonderful things we remember about her. Yet, I have never asked another Lester Potts about what motivates him to continue to love a woman who is not really the woman he loves, but only a memory of that woman.

I should know these things, but it's difficult to ask myself such hard questions. And if I did, Lester might just tell me lies. Did I mention that Lester often lies?

Group

I had no interest in going to the AA meeting, but the court had made it part of my probation, so I had to show up. I had hoped that I could blend in the background somewhere and that no one would want to know why I was there, but the set-up seemed designed to provoke "sharing" among the participants.

I took a seat on one of the fold-up chairs that had been set up in a circle in the church basement. I was the last to come in, but Father Gregorius beamed at me like I was the Prodigal returned to the fold. "Ah," he said to the assembled, "we have someone new to the group tonight. Please introduce yourself and say a few words about what brought you here. Just what you feel comfortable with."

The priest was wearing a cardigan over his clerical collar. The other people in group looked pretty much like the people I'd met in my prior AA meetings. Of course, they were all younger than I was. There were a couple of forty-ish blue collar guys with shaved heads, a teenage girl in a pink miniskirt, a motherly-looking woman who was knitting, and a black guy in a ratty green army great coat. They all looked happy to meet me. I tried to pretend that I was happy, too.

"My name is Gene," I said. "I've been an abstainer for thirty years, off and on." I could have said for sixty years. That's how old I was, but people got nervous when they heard it. They didn't want to know about anything that had happened that long ago.

Father Gregorius spoke up. "Gene, the first step in the healing process is to recognize that you are an abstainer. We're not here to judge you. All of us have gone through periods in which we refused the drugs that we were given. But with the help of others, we've all been able to stand strong and recognize that the drugs help make us better people."

"I recognize that I've been weak." I was lying, but I tried to flash everyone a big grin.

Father Gregorius turned toward the girl. "It's easy to tell ourselves that we can stand on our own two feet without any help. Sometimes we just want to push everyone else away. Miranda, maybe it would be helpful to Gene if you told him why you stopped using."

Miranda offered us a brilliant smile. "Well, my mother died and, I don't really know why, but it sort of got on my nerves that everybody seemed to be taking it so well. I know now that it was better that way, but, well, it irritated me that everybody kept on smiling and saying Mom had gone to a better place and, really, the worst thing was that I was smiling, too, and saying the same things and I kept wondering why I didn't, you know, feel something more, well, deeper about it, so I started throwing my medication in the trash although I kept telling everyone that I was still high, but I really wasn't."

"And what happened after that," Father Gregorius prompted.

Miranda gave us that smile again, but I noticed that she was pulling at one of her finger nails and that a small line of red had appeared inside the cuticle. "Yeah, well, I started to feel awful. I mean I started to question everything. I started to wonder why I had to work the job at the diner that I was given after high school and why I had to wear the uniform with the short skirt that they gave me. I was even starting to wonder if I loved the husband I had been assigned."

Someone in the group coughed. Father Gregorius held Miranda's hand, the one that was bleeding. "And, Miranda," he asked, "did your stubbornness cause you to fail to attend to your duties?"

Miranda looked at the floor. "Yes, Father, it did. I stopped attending services. I think that's how Social Services found out about me. They sent a couple of Social Workers out to see me and after we had talked they found a rehabilitation camp where I could stay for a while."

"And has that made a difference in your life?"

"Oh, yes, Father, I've been using my drugs every day and I feel much happier. I never want to go to that dark place in my life, again."

Father Gregorius looked triumphant. He seemed ready to move on to my story, but the black guy spoke up first.

"My name is Roberto and I've been in Abstainers Anonymous for five years. I started coming after I got back from my military service. It was pretty bad over there. I don't want to give away any secrets, but there were times when my unit took big losses. And the ordnance that they used over there…well, you never could find enough left of anybody who got hit by one of those smart shells to bury."

Father Gregorius interrupted. "Stay on point, Roberto, we want to know what brought you here, but no one wants to hear the details of what happened to you in Belarus. You were serving the state. You did what you had to do."

Roberto's expression didn't change. "Well, what I wanted to say was that I was sitting around the mess tent one morning and I was looking around at the other guys and I realized that I didn't know any of them. They were all replacements. All the guys I had come up with were gone. And I suddenly had this… like a flash… a vision of a guy I had been friends with and his face was sort of melting away and his body was… just blown apart. And I just stopped eating. I don't know why."

"Were you taking your drugs?"

"Sure. And I felt good. I mean, I was feeling fine. But for some reason, I just started wondering why I was feeling so good when everybody I knew was dead."

"But you didn't tell anyone about your feelings, did you?"

"No, I didn't want anyone to think that I was letting the other guys down. I just started to taper off. I dropped the anti-depressant first and then I quit on the anti-anxiety pill. I never quit using the energy medication, though."

"Were you able to continue fighting?"

"Yeah, I was still one of the best. At least, I thought I was. Then one day I was sitting on my cot and I had one of those Tasers that we used for civilians and I put it to my head and started thinking about what it might do to my mind. Somehow I had the idea that it might clear up my thoughts, that I might start thinking straight, again. Anyway, some of the guys grabbed me and the next thing you know I was stateside in a camp."

"That's where you were treated for Post-Traumatic Stress Syndrome, right?

"Yeah, and they taught me about the dangers of self-non-medication. I guess that's what I was doing. But I'm back on the program now and I feel fine. I sure do."

"That's great, Roberto." Father Gregorius put his hand on Roberto's shoulder before he turned toward me.

"So, now, Gene, maybe you would tell us what has brought you here?"

"Well," I said, "I'm on probation."

Father Gregorius didn't stop grinning. "Please, Gene, would you share what happened to you? I assure you that we're only concerned about your well-being here. What was your criminal sin?"

"Remembering. It's a class three offense. I was remembering what it was like when I was a kid. Unfortunately, I made the mistake of sharing what I remembered with a co-worker."

No one in the group responded. I guess they were listening, but maybe they didn't know anything about why the state didn't like people talking about the old days.

"Hasn't your doctor given you something for that, Gene?"

"Yeah, I'm supposed to take this blue pill every day. But it doesn't work the way it's supposed to. I still remember things, but the pill just jumbles things up. I told my doctor that I thought, maybe, if I stopped taking my other pills, the blue one would work, but he wouldn't let me do that. Then they tested me and found out I had stopped taking the other pills on my own. I had to go to the therapy institute. I did six months there before they let me out. That was three weeks ago."

"I have to ask you this, Gene: are you really ready to be saved? Are you really ready to walk the straight and narrow?"

"Sure, Father, I'm ready to re-join society. I'm back on my prescriptions. Hell, some days I can't even remember my own name."

"Gene, let me speak frankly. You seem a little down tonight. Are you sure that you're being compliant with your pharmaceutical regime?"

I'm sure that Father Gregorius could see that I was sweating. "Really," I said, "I'm very happy right now. I don't think I could be any happier and I'm looking forward to getting back to work. I've got some big projects I want to ...."

My voice had trailed off. I wasn't sure what to say next. I had dumped the pills I had been given when I had been released from the institute. I just wanted to be sure that what I remembered was real and not messed up by everything that the state had taught people since the Great Cleansing.

I was just a kid when the world had changed. Whenever I wanted to talk to a counselor about anything that had happened then like the public executions or the street snipers he would just give me another pill and tell me it was all in my mind. Nothing like that had really gone on. I could check the history articles on the internet.

Father Gregorius moved back to a desk at the side of the room. I thought I saw him touch something underneath the writing top.

"Ten minute break, everyone," the Father announced. "there's water on the table over there, if you need to refresh your meds."

I drifted outside. I had a few minutes to stare at the ruins across the street before my Probation Officer showed up. Walking next to him was a Social Worker wearing the usual powder blue jumpsuit. When the SWs had first appeared thirty years ago my friends had called them the Happiness Squad.

I guess I shouldn't have been surprised that they showed up so quickly. The government had its offices in the church.

19

My probation officer seemed as happy as usual even if a little apologetic. "Gene, we've had some complaints about you. We need to take you in for testing."

I shrugged. "Did you know that there used to be a library over there? It had hundreds of thousands of books printed on paper and you could check one out anytime you wanted to. You didn't have to get permission from anyone. It was my favorite place when I was a kid."

I saw a look of disgust pass across the face of the Social Worker. "Man," he said, "you really are a hard case."

"He's just off his meds," my probation officer told him. "Gene's doing some important work for us. He's got some scientific skills that are very useful to us, so we'd like to get him back after he's been treated."

The SW patted the taser on his belt. "Maybe Gene here is too far gone to ever come back. Not everybody does, you know."

After the SW shoved a few pills into my mouth and made sure I swallowed them he walked me around the back of the church where there was a loading dock for the buses that took people away to the desert. By the time I reached the institute, I was sane again, and very happy.

Drone

I flew drones in the last war. I set a record for hours flown, which I couldn't talk about and I was awarded a couple of medals, which I had to keep secret. No one knew anything about me except the government, but they must have thought I was a pretty good pilot because after I left the service they recruited me to fly their time machine.

As you might have guessed, there weren't a lot of people who knew about the project. There was Dr. Hyatt plus his entourage of junior scientists, graduate students, and technicians, and there were all the generals and spook types who kept the goings-on funded, and there was me. I didn't even have a back-up.

I worked out of a control room that had been set up in the corner of a hangar on a military air base. The shed was huge, but my space was minimal. There was just enough room for me, my ergonomic chair and the bank of instruments that I used to guide the damn thing when it went back into the past.

The generals and spooks watched the happenings in real time back at their offices in Langley or Foggy Bottom. I never met any of the brass and I never saw any of them make an on-site visit.

There were about twenty staff members on-site. I knew most of them by name, but I wasn't close to any of them. Dr. Ponder was the friendliest of the lot. I was always de-briefed after we ran a mission and Dr. Ponder was usually the staff member who took my report after a mission.

Dr. Ponder had introduced herself as Cindy at our first meeting, so I didn't think it was over-familiar of me to call her by that name. She called me Stan.

Cindy was a petite brunette with big brown sympathetic eyes. Anyway, they looked sympathetic to me. They were certainly brown.

She had a nice sense of humor. By that, I mean that she laughed at my jokes. I never tried to dial our relationship up to "let's go out somewhere for drinks." because she wore a gold band on her left hand and also because I was still smarting from a divorce that was in no way "amicable."

The time machine looked very much like a military drone. I'm sure that they had simply adapted a drone frame to carry the machinery that Dr. Hyatt had created. It had a torpedo-like fuselage, a V-shaped tail and two small wing-mounted propellers. It was fitted out with various devices for measuring, recording and generally sniffing out whatever it encountered.

Don't ask me how the drone worked. First of all, everything about the project was on a need-to-know basis, so no one was going to sit me down in a classroom and diagram the whole thing out. Second, the little I overheard didn't make any sense.

I have a degree in aviation engineering and I'm familiar with the technical jargon that gets used when tech geeks talk aeronautics, but I don't have enough knowledge of quantum physics - actually, I don't have any knowledge of quantum physics - to allow me to have the slightest idea what Dr. Hyatt meant when he dropped a few gems about neutrino anomalies or whatever.

I do know that the drone required an enormous amount of energy. You could tell that by the big cables that ran into the back of the hanger where there was an array of equipment that looked like the control room of a nuclear power plant. Whenever we sent the drone out, there were a few technicians back there checking the dials and looking very anxious.

What I did was pretty simple. Whenever there was a mission I would take my seat in the control room and wait for the scientists to activate the time travel drive, or whatever they called it. This was often the most exciting part of the mission for me because I always got a thrill when the drone gave off a green flash and disappeared.

After a few seconds, a scene would appear on the screen of my control panel. Most of the time, I would be looking at a flat, Great Plains sort of landscape. The time travel part of the mission moved the drone temporally, not spatially. We were based in the mid-west, so, when the drone arrived in the past, what we saw was usually very similar to what we had started with, just a couple of thousand years or so in the past.

If everything looked good for take-off, I'd move my joystick and the drone would head off into the prehistoric skies. If I spotted a problem, I could abort and the drone would immediately return to the present.

On one occasion, I had found myself staring into the face of bull bison with a herd of a hundred thousand other bison lined up behind him. On another trip, the drone showed up about a hundred yards from a tornado. I called the drone back both times. Those had been easy decisions for me, even though it must have cost the taxpayers about a million bucks just for our drone to be in the past for thirty seconds.

Once I was in the air, I followed Dr. Hyatt's instructions. He would say things like "go to two thousand feet and check out those foothills on the right," and I'd execute. I was never sure what he was looking for, but where the drone went was his call.

Maybe that's why I liked the landings best. It was my responsibility to bring the drone back to the coordinates where it had started. This wasn't always the easiest job. Every mission took place in a different time period and each time I flew there was a new geographical situation at the landing site.

I had an indefinite tour of duty. Usually I worked a ten hour shift, but if a problem cropped up, I might be at the hangar for forty-eight hours without going home. I didn't fly missions every day, but each mission required so much prep time that I often had to call my wife at the last moment to tell her I would be getting home late again. I think that this was one of the causes of my divorce. Vanna, my ex, didn't like it when I was away for so long and the fact that I couldn't tell her what I was doing while I was away because it was a matter of national security only made things worse.

I was sort of like a super hero with a secret identity. When my wife asked me what I did at work, I had to tell her that I did some, you know, pilot stuff. I certainly wasn't allowed to say that I was changing our idea of how the universe worked.

I had been with the project for almost two years when I pulled my twentieth mission. For this flight, the engineering team had installed an extra bank of controls in my office cockpit. I was told that Dr. Hyatt wanted to test out the possibility that the drone could switch time periods in mid-flight.

Chu, one of the technicians, went over the instruments with me a week before we were to launch and I was able to run several simulated flights on our computer, so, by the day we were to go, I felt like I wouldn't have any trouble with the drone.

I had the control screen on while everyone went through the pre-flight protocols. Dr. Hyatt was standing in front of the drone making notes on a clipboard. Behind him I could see several technicians at their stations along the back wall.

A green flash appeared on the drone screen just as the sound of a blast ripped through the hangar. As the window shattered behind me I felt a piece of glass slash across my left arm. I dropped to the floor and crawled back to my door that opened onto the hangar floor.

When I raised my head to peek over the shards sticking up from the window frame, I saw that several of the project staff had been injured. One of the technicians was lying on his back on the floor grasping his leg. Another technician was moaning as he limped toward the staff offices.

The first thing I looked for was fire, but I didn't see any flames or smoke. I checked the hangar over and I noticed that there seemed to be less damage than I would have expected from the force of the blast.

I didn't see any breach in the walls and the drone was still upright in the middle of the room.

As I tried to remember our emergency procedures I realized that I didn't see Dr. Hyatt anywhere. I didn't know where the explosion had started, but I was afraid that it had occurred right about where Dr. Hyatt had been standing.

But that couldn't be right. If the blast had hit Dr. Hyatt, it must have come from the area around the drone and I could see that the drone was still upright at the other end of the hangar

While I was sorting out the sequence of events, I noticed something moving on the drone screen.

I turned around and was presented with the image of Dr. Hyatt waving his hands above his head. I was trying to figure out how Dr. Hyatt had gotten in front of the drone when it hit me that the scene behind Dr. Hyatt was not the interior of our building, but, rather, an endless stretch of grasslands.

There was one drone inside the hangar and another out there on the prairie with Dr. Hyatt.

There was no way to hear Dr. Hyatt because the drone wasn't set up to transmit sound. You didn't need to hear anything when you were flying at several thousand feet.

The staff was busy out on the hangar floor. Some people were tending to the injured technicians. Another group had gathered at the exit. One of the technicians was pounding his hand on the steel door and shouting, "Let us out of here, goddammit!"

When Dr. Witte, the associate project director, trotted by, I shouted, "We've got to help Dr. Hyatt! He's been sent into the past!"

Dr. Witte gave me a look like he wondered if I had hit my head, but he came in and took a glance at the screen. When he recognized Dr. Hyatt and figured out where Dr. Hyatt was, or perhaps I should say when Dr. Hyatt was, he gasped.

"But how are we seeing him?" he asked, although I don't think that he was expecting an answer from me. "I mean, the drone's sitting here in our time. How can it exist both here and in the past simultaneously?"

He seemed to be working out something in his head. He turned to me and remarked, "I suppose the fact that the same object can be in two places at different times doesn't contradict any of the laws of thermodynamics. It's not like we're creating matter, here."

I told him I agreed. I did that mostly because I had no idea about what he had said. I was actually thinking to myself, "I guess I should have expected that a scientist would be more concerned with figuring out the physics of the situation than in rescuing his colleague."

A moment later, the intercom summoned us to a meeting. Everybody in the hangar stopped what they were doing and headed for the conference room. Even the people at the exit gave up trying to get out. They left the door and took their seats in front of a large projection screen.

Someone in a uniform with two stars on his shoulder addressed the staff. He expressed his sympathy to everyone, particularly those of us who had been suffered injuries in the line of duty. However, he said, because of concerns for national security none of us would be allowed to leave the building until Washington said so.

This didn't go over well. There was a lot of muttering and someone shouted at the screen, "We've got people here who've been hurt! They need emergency medical care!"

The general didn't show any concern. "Life-threatening injuries will be considered on a case by case basis. You'll have to treat less serious problems yourself. Nobody comes in and nobody goes out until we've got a handle on this situation."

The general then asked whether Dr. Hyatt was in the audience. Dr. Witte looked around before answering. I'm sure the bastard was considering whether he should share his information about Dr. Hyatt with the rest of the staff, or whether he should ask for a private meeting and disclose it only to the generals and spooks, but, at last, Dr. Witte cleared his throat and offered, "Dr. Hyatt is no longer physically in the building. However, it appears that he is alive in the past."

This provoked more murmuring among the staff. Dr. Witte may have thought that his news about Dr. Hyatt sounded implausible, so he handed off to me. "Stan, tell them what you saw on the drone screen."

I told the general that I had seen Dr. Hyatt standing in what appeared to be a prairie and that he seemed to be trying to make contact with the drone.

Someone behind the general asked, "What were the time parameters for the new mission?"

"We were going back 5000 years," Dr. Witte responded, "plus or minus a century."

The general backed away and introduced a panel of four men and a woman. They proceeded to interrogate us about what had happened in the time period immediately before the accident. Some of the questions to Dr. Witte and the other scientists were so complex that I could only get a general idea of what was being asked.

After some give and take with the members of the panel, Dr. Witte asserted himself. "We have a great opportunity here," he announced. "Previously, we required incredible amounts of electrical power to transmit our drone into another time. Now, we have created a portal into the past. I believe that our efforts should be directed to stabilizing this entrance. If we can create a permanent gate to the past we can enter and leave almost without any expenditure of energy."

This seemed to provoke one of the panelists, the woman who had been introduced as Dr. Helen Polanski. "You have used the metaphor of a portal, or gate, to describe the relationship that currently exists between space/time at your facility and the point in space/time where Dr. Hyatt exists in the past. But isn't this the wrong metaphor? Isn't what you've described more like a wound than gate? Isn't it likely that this hole in time/space will close in on itself in order to end the paradoxical existence of the drone which is occupying two places in time?"

"We are monitoring the drone closely," Dr. Witte said. "We have not seen any changes in either drone since the explosion established the gate between the two points in time."

Dr. Polanski persisted. "You are just one observer on the train platform, Doctor. From your observation point, everything may appear completely normal. But there may be time distortions at your location which are so subtle that you do not see them occurring."

At this point, the general came back on the screen and cut off debate. He told us that there were sufficient emergency rations in the hangar to last our staff for several weeks and he assured us that the government was doing all it could to get us home.

There were a few more pleas from the staff, mostly of the "can't I call my loved ones?" sort, but the general remained implacable. Our phones were cut off. The military would tell our families only that we were safe and that we would be out of contact for a while.

The screen defaulted to a DOD emblem. I sat thinking about the situation for a few minutes until Cindy took a seat beside me and asked if I was hurt. "There's blood on the sleeve of your shirt. Don't you want to get some treatment for that?"

Cindy walked me over to an aid station that a couple of the grad students had set up. She waited while Ken Wilson put antiseptic on my cuts and wrapped a bandage around my arm. He also gave me some ibuprofen and told me to come back if the pain got any worse. After I thanked him, he said, "I guess I should have gone to med school instead of Cal Tech."

I told Cindy that I needed some coffee and she came with me to the break room. We sat for a few minutes while she told me about the theories circulating among the staff about what had happened. Some ascribed the explosion to the new equipment on the drone. One theory was that the particle beam had been knocked off line when one of the techs was changing the overhead lights. A few theories involved dark plots by "the powers that be" to eliminate the program and everyone associated with it.

In the middle of our conversation Cindy put her coffee mug down with a thud and said, "Please tell me that we're going to get out of here alive. Tell me I'm going to see my family again."

I assured her that everything would be fine. I didn't hold out much hope for getting Dr. Hyatt back, but I pointed out that no one else had suffered any serious injury, that we had plenty of food and water, that we still had power, and that we were only a few feet from a major military facility full of billions of dollars' worth of equipment. Cindy shook her head while I talked, but she didn't disagree with anything I said.

When I got back to my office, I checked on Dr. Hyatt. He was sitting in front of the drone's camera with a look of dejection and hopelessness. The sky behind him was beginning to darken. I wondered if he would be able to survive a night in 3000 B.C.

Dr. Hyatt let me keep a cot in my office that I used during delays in the drone countdowns. I found it a useful place to rest or read a detective novel while I waited for Dr. Hyatt to put the launch back into "go" status.

After I had swept the broken glass from my office I plopped down on the thin mattress and looked at the ceiling while I went over the day's events in my mind. I didn't mean to fall asleep, but I did.

The drone screen was completely black when Dr. Witte shook me awake. I don't know how long I had been asleep, but I felt like I hadn't gotten any rest at all. "Come with me to the conference room," he whispered, "there's been some new developments."

I took a place at the table opposite Dr. Witte. Cindy was there and also Drs. Lee and Rodriquez, two members of the scientific team. Someone had set up a whiteboard that showed what appeared to be a diagram of the hangar floor. The center of the diagram was marked "drone" and there were names written at various distances from it.

Dr. Hyatt's name was written the closest to the center. Someone had put a checkmark with a red magic marker above his name. I understood that, but I didn't know why there were two other check marks, one next to "Santoro" and one next to "Johnson." I recognized these as the names of two of the technicians.

Dr. Witte started the meeting with the announcement that Santoro and Johnson had disappeared. "In case you're wondering," he said, "the security doors are still locked, so I don't think they slipped out for a smoke."

Dr. Lee asked if the building had been thoroughly searched. Dr. Witte waved the question away and continued, "I had a rather disturbing conversation with some of the staff this morning. Some of the electricians were standing back near the generator station and when I walked by, they asked if we had changed the schedule for the new launch. I talked with them for a few minutes while being very careful about what I said to them and I became convinced that they had no memory of the events of yesterday."

"Shit." I think I was the one who said that, but it could have been any of the others.

Dr. Witte didn't even look back. He stood and walked to the whiteboard. "If I'm right about the positions of everyone yesterday at the time of the blast, Santoro and Johnson were standing here and here, just behind Dr. Hyatt. The electricians were down at the end of the building about a hundred feet from the drone. The three techs on the propulsion team were back here about the same distance away, but in the opposite direction."

"I was with Ponder, Lee, and Rodriquez in the scientific instruments section getting ready to start collecting data, so we were about 100 to 150 feet from the drone." Dr. Witte circled a room of offices on the other side of the drone. "Wilson and his team of graduate students were a little closer than we were. They were in the life sciences section over here, that is, about 20 feet closer to the drone than the instruments section."

Dr. Witte looked back at me, "And our lonely pilot was in his control room down here in the corner of the hangar, maybe 100 yards from the drone."

Cindy spoke up, "So you're saying there was some sort of time distortion and that it is affecting the people closest to the drone."

"Yes, I think that we must consider the possibility that one of the effects of this distortion is that time has reversed itself for some of our staff and that one consequence of this reversal is memory loss." Dr. Witte smiled. It looked more like a wince.

Everyone was quiet. We had all shown signs of anxiety before Dr. Witte spoke, but now I was seeing panic. Then, Dr. Witte cleared his throat and everything got worse.

He continued, "I believe that the effects of this distortion have manifested themselves first to those closest to the blast. I say 'first,' because, as of now, we have no data to establish how great this effect is. It may well be that everyone here will be affected eventually. If so, we constitute the staff members who will probably have the longest time to work on reversing the effects."

Dr. Rodriquez exploded, "We've got to get out of here immediately. We've got to talk to Washington and convince them to open the doors, now."

Dr. Witte made some desultory marks on the board. "I relayed this information to Washington this morning. They promised to get back to me as soon as possible. Since then, they haven't contacted us and I haven't been able to contact them. All that seems to have happened, judging by the security cameras, is that the MPs who were manning the security gate in front of the hangar have moved back and have been replaced by a company of marines and several armored vehicles."

I said, "It's like they think we've caught some sort of disease, that we're carrying the time plague."

Dr. Witte agreed. "That's it exactly. So you can imagine that they're very scared out there. Still, they haven't shut down the power and they haven't started shooting, yet, so maybe we've got a chance to think of some way out of this."

The scientists began talking about the physics of the situation and my eyes started to glaze over. All I could make out was that some of the scientists thought that the time distortion might be reversed if the drone could be called back from the past. There was some talk of a "displacement," that is, that once the drone from the past and the drone in the present were re-united physically the time portal would close.

I guess everybody noticed that I wasn't adding anything to the discussion, so Dr. Witte suggested that I return to the drone control room. He promised to text me when they had figured out what we could do.

On my way out of the meeting, I ran into Chu and some of the other technicians. Chu called out to me, "Hey, Stan, what's happening? Our shift is up and it seems that we're on lockdown. We can't go home. Are we in some sort of emergency status? And where's Dr. Hyatt?"

I wasn't sure what I could tell them. Saying that there had been a terrible accident that was causing everyone to lose their memories didn't seem like the best way to approach the situation. I was fishing around for some sort of story that would calm everyone down when Dr. Witte came out of the conference room and told Chu to get back to work. Dr. Witte had never demonstrated any human relations skills before, so I wasn't surprised that he had put his foot in it so forcefully.

The technicians circled Dr. Witte and began to demand to know what was going on.

Dr. Witte raised his voice and said that no one could leave the building, that there was an emergency situation and he didn't have time to brief everyone about what was going on, but that Washington had given him full authority over the project, and blah, blah.

I left Dr. Witte to try to straighten out the brouhaha that he had created and walked back to the control room. The drone was showing a beautiful sunrise somewhere back in the past. As the day grew lighter, I searched the screen for evidence that Dr. Hyatt was still in the land of the living. Yes, there was a human figure in front of the drone. Then there was another and then a third.

"Shit." This time I knew that it me who said it. The sun was getting higher and I could see Dr. Hyatt making motions at the drone. Beside him Santoro and Johnson were stamping their feet. It must have been cold out there on the plains.

I watched for a minute before I sent a text message to Dr. Witte: SANTORO AND JOHNSON ALIVE ON SCREEN IN PAST.

Dr. Witte trotted over to the drone control room at a surprisingly brisk pace for someone who was in his late fifties and a bit overweight. He glanced at the screen and blurted out, "My God, the drone's created some sort of backwash that's dragging people into the past."

Turning toward me, he said, "We've got to move on this displacement attempt. We might not even have an hour left. Get everything ready with your controls."

I asked, "Wasn't this just about losing our memories?"

Dr. Witte replied, "The effects are worse than I thought. I assumed that everyone in the hangar might be affected. Now, I'm wondering if we pulled the plug at the bottom of the sea and the whole ocean is going to drain away."

He started out of the room, but stopped for a last look at the screen. "I didn't think I'd finish my scientific career throwing flint spears at bison, but that may happen."

I went back to work getting my controls on line. As I ran through my checklist for a drone flight, I considered what my chances for survival would be if I was sucked into prehistory. Not good was my assessment.

On the other hand, I remembered that Dr. Lee had said that the drone reappearing in the present might cause some sort of nuclear event that would leave a smoking crater where the hangar had been. Dr. Witte had assured us that this couldn't happen, but maybe that was another miscalculation.

I could see from my booth that the technicians and scientists were taking up posts on the hangar floor. It looked like we were proceeding with the launch. Dr. Witte must have brow beat the technicians into going back to their jobs. Maybe, he had come up with a particularly convincing lie.

As the countdown went forward, I became more anxious. I wrapped my hand around the drone's flight stick for a good twenty minutes before the mission was supposed to start and I didn't let go as the countdown progressed.

We passed five minutes to the jump. I could feel sweat on the back of my neck. Four minutes, three minutes…then the power went off.

The hangar went dark for a few seconds before the emergency generator kicked in. We had practiced for this situation before, so I knew that there would be a lag while the computers rebooted and went through their internal check lists.

The system was designed to allow just enough light for people to find the exits. There were floods over the front doors which, I assumed, were still locked, and glowing strips along the walls to point you in the right direction. A red flasher was sweeping the hangar floor every couple of seconds and an alarm was sounding from speakers mounted on each wall.

I couldn't see far into the hangar although I could make out shapes moving around and I could hear shouting. I was wondering whether our attempt to launch the drone had overloaded the grid, or whether the government had cut the power to the hangar. Maybe they had monitored what we were doing and had decided to make sure we couldn't get the drone away.

While I was trying to think over my options, Cindy staggered through my office door. She took a few steps inside before she fell to her knees. She looked at me and moaned, "They're all gone. I saw them disappear. There was a flash of green and a little pop and they were gone."

"Who's gone?" I asked.

"The guys in the back who run the machinery, the electrical technicians. They were just standing there and then they disappeared."

"How about Dr. Witte and the rest of the staff?"

"I don't know. The lights went out and I lost sight of everyone. I tried to get out the hangar door, but it was locked. Then I turned around and came looking for someone who could help me."

"I wish I could. I think we're screwed."

"Don't say that. There's got to be some way out of here. Or maybe we can call Washington."

"We tried that before. They don't want to hear anything about what's going on here."

Cindy glared at me. "Look, buddy, I don't know who you are, but I was hoping you could help, not give me all this defeatist crap."

That silenced me. I really didn't know what to say after that.

Cindy had pulled herself upright by the time power came back on. Both Cindy and I gaped at the drone screen when it lit up and showed Dr. Hyatt and most of the staff waving at the camera.

"Where is everyone?" Cindy asked.

"They're in the past," I told her. I stopped myself from adding, "And we'll be there too before long."

The main lights came up in the hangar. Dr. Witte was standing by the drone. I could see a couple of the other scientists milling around behind him. Dr. Witte looked about as despondent as Dr. Hyatt had looked when I saw him sitting in the grass in the past.

I felt sorry for Cindy and Dr. Witte and everybody else. I was hoping that whatever had caused the time disruption had missed me and that I could avoid a one way trip to 3000 BCE. If I didn't show any effects after a few days, maybe Washington would open the doors and let me out.

And what about those people who were stuck in pre-history. At least, they were together. If they could get a fire started, they probably wouldn't die of exposure and they might be able to organize a defense against predators. If I remembered what I'd been told in the briefings correctly, there were Native Americans living to the east and to the southwest of the Plains. Maybe, they could find other humans and join up with them.

"I think that I'd better consult with Dr. Witte," Cindy said. "By the way, I'm Dr. Cynthia Ponder, but, please, call me Cindy."

"I'm Stan. I'm a drone pilot."

"Great. We'll certainly need you when we get this project up and running."

35

I watched as Cindy left and walked over to Dr. Witte.

I tried to check out the drone controls, but I kept glancing back at the screen. People were moving in and out of the picture. It seemed like they were proceeding with some purpose. I thought that I could see smoke rising in the background.

While I watched, I started scratching my right arm. Damn, if there wasn't a bandage on it. How did that get there? I'm of the school that says quick is better than slow, so I ripped the tape off even though the adhesive snagged enough of my hair that I had to muffle a scream.

So this is what the control room looked like. I was looking forward to working on the project, even though I had my doubts about whether anyone could fly a drone into the past.

When I turned around to look for my waste basket so I could get rid of the tape I'd removed I realized that the hangar was empty. This could be a problem. I hoped that Dr. Hyatt hadn't made some mistake and left the new guy behind when everyone else went home for the day. I had told my wife I'd be home by five and I didn't want to be late. I'd get an earful from Vanna if I missed another one of her special dinners.

The Coat

After the waitress with green hair had served our lunches, Arthur directed my attention to the coat he was wearing. In appearance, it was a standard looking, khaki-colored, below the knee length trench coat with the straps across the shoulder. It differed from the usual model only in that the buttons down the front weren't made of plastic, but had a metallic sheen. However, Arthur was convinced that the coat was something more than this.

"I first believed that it was some sort of survival suit for an alien life form, but now I think that it may have another purpose." This was one of the most nonsensical statements I had ever heard anyone make, but Arthur spoke without any sign of embarrassment.

I answered him with a less-than-polite "Something like keeping out the rain, I assume," before continuing my examination of the eggplant something that sat on a dish mere inches from my defenseless taste buds. Now I had another reason to regret agreeing to join Arthur at his favorite vegetarian restaurant.

Arthur and I had met about a decade ago when we both taught in the English department at the local university. Arthur handled 20th Century British Literature and I was a specialist in British literature of the 19th century. As our courses dovetailed, we met periodically to make sure that our curricula didn't overlap.

Of course, we had also discussed our respective views on British literature. I had always enjoyed the give and take of our conversations. I disagreed, for example, with his assertion that Coleridge was a greater poet than Wordsworth. He, in turn, thought that I was too dismissive about the merits of contemporary poetry. I wouldn't have described us as dear friends, but we had had what I considered to be an amiable relationship.

Now we were both retired from teaching. When we met at academic gatherings at the university we always made an effort to talk, but these conversations were never as intense as the discussions we had once had.

Today we had run into each other in the stacks of the university library. This was the first time I had spoken with him in the six months since the funeral of his wife and, as I felt somewhat guilty about not making any effort to see him, I had immediately accepted an invitation to join him for lunch.

I had assumed that he needed some company. Now I was wondering if grief and loneliness had affected his mind.

"I'm serious," he said and sent an intense gaze in my direction. Perhaps he had been following my line of thought.

I considered saying, "No one is more serious than a madman and, sadly, Arthur, that's exactly what it appears you've become," but, instead, I pushed my plate away from me and looked directly at Arthur. "Okay, Arthur, tell me what makes you believe that your trench coat is something other than a trench coat. I mean, it looks pretty unremarkable. It probably says London Fog on the label inside. Does it have a zip out lining?"

"It does not have a zip out lining," Arthur responded in tones that seemed encased in icicles. "In fact, I have no idea what is inside this coat because I cannot take it off although I have been wearing it for at least a month."

"That's ridiculous," I said. "I mean, to begin with, that is the most unhygienic thing I have ever heard. Aren't you bathing?"

"I don't need to bathe. So far as I can tell, the coat keeps me completely clean." Arthur leaned across the table and spoke in a lower voice. "It also disposes entirely of my, uh, bodily waste."

"Do you mean to say that you haven't, well, visited a bathroom in a month? That you've just gone in your coat?"

"Exactly." He said this with an attitude of defiance, as though he knew that I wouldn't want to believe him.

"Phew," I said. "If that were true, I wouldn't want to be sitting across this table from you. You would be reeking to high heaven."

"But you don't smell a thing do you, Bryce? Indeed, the only odor I have noted while wearing this coat is something like a slight rosemary scent, which is actually quite pleasant."

I shrugged. "So what else is this marvelous coat doing for you, Arthur?"

"Well, for one thing," he replied, "I don't have to breathe, anymore. It seems to handle that whole respiration thing for me."

"That's rid..." I stopped. I would have to think of a new phrase if I was going to continue this conversation. Ridiculous was clearly inadequate to describe what Arthur was telling me. I wondered if the use of "bat shit crazy" would be more appropriate.

Arthur pulled a small rectangular mirror from one of his pockets. He held in under his nose for a few seconds and then tilted it in my direction. "Do you see?" he asked.

"See what?"

"Do you see any fog on the mirror that would indicate the presence of breath?"

"No," I agreed, "but I'm not sure that proves the accuracy of your observation. You have to be breathing. Everyone breathes."

"Everyone requires oxygen. Breathing is just one way of obtaining it. I believe that this coat supplies whatever oxygen I need directly to my lungs.

"Uh, huh. And does it let you fly, too?"

"Don't be ridiculous," Arthur snapped. Now he was saying it. He paused and turned back to his plate to take a few bites from a substance that looked suspiciously like Soylent Green. When he had finished chewing, he took another look at me. "Did you know that for the last few years I've suffered from severe back pain associated with a herniated disc? My doctor prescribed Vicodin which I refused to take. Instead I've gotten by on aspirin and copious amounts of red wine."

"I didn't know that, Arthur. I'm sorry to hear...."

He cut me off. "I haven't felt so much as a twinge out of my back since I've been wearing this coat. More than that, my acid reflux is gone and my senses have improved dramatically. As you can see, I'm not wearing my glasses. I don't need to."

"You sound like an infomercial."

"Say what you want to, Bryce, but I feel like I'm twenty, again"

You can't reason with a lunatic. I knew that, but I soldiered on, determined to be logical in the face of illogic. "Surely, wearing a coat must cause you serious inconvenience. For example, you look a bit strange sitting at a booth inside a restaurant with your coat still on. And how do you sleep in it? Isn't that uncomfortable?"

"I don't sleep," Arthur said. "I reset. I close my eyes and, in a few minutes, I come back refreshed and alert. The time I've saved by not sleeping has allowed me to catch up on my reading and to start writing my book on the poetry of Michael Donaghy, which, as you know, I always said I was going to start, but never got to." He raised his eyebrows. "So tell me, Bryce, what are *you* doing in retirement?"

I pushed whatever it was on my plate around with my fork. There was a Thai fusion bistro down the street. It looked like I would be having an early dinner there. "Okay, Arthur, how did you get this amazing coat? I hope it didn't require signing away your soul."

"Lost and found," Arthur said. "I got it right here. During that on again off again spell of cold weather in the fall, I left my own coat somewhere. I thought I might have left it here, so I checked in the back room. I found this one instead. The owner urged me to take it. He said that it had been there for weeks and that no one had claimed it. I tried it on and it seemed to fit, so I took it. During the course of that day, the coat's properties manifested themselves. I've been wearing it ever since then."

I had been growing depressed about my friend's evident madness. Even so, I had to laugh out loud when he told me where he had found the coat. I couldn't imagine any reason for an alien to visit Murray's Vegetarian Restaurant. The place had started up in the sixties as a sort of dining commune. Now, it seemed like a social club for aging socialists. I could see a lot of grey hair and dangly ear-rings.

"That must have been one careless alien to have left his coat at a vegetarian restaurant," I remarked.

Arthur snapped back, "I'm not surprised that an alien would patronize a vegetarian restaurant. I'm sure that any society that could manage space travel would have risen to a cultural level that didn't require it to send animal life to the slaughterhouse."

Lifting another forkful of green mush to his mouth, Arthur looked out the window at the bored drivers in a line of cars stuck in traffic. He seemed to be mulling over what to say next. "But I admit that I've asked myself why an alien would abandon this coat, if it were, in fact, a survival suit. If we assume that this coat was necessary to deal with earth's environment, why would its owner depart without it? That's a question that has made me reconsider my initial hypothesis. At first, it seemed like the coat was all about security. Now, I'm beginning to think it's all about transformation."

"Transformation? What are you saying?"

He looked back at me. "I feel different in this coat, Bryce. As I'm sure you know I'm not in the best of health. I thought that I had had reconciled myself to the mortification of the flesh, but wearing this coat has allowed me to do things that I haven't done in years. Today I walked from my house to the art museum. That's about five miles. I didn't lose my balance. I wasn't short of breath. I didn't feel tired. If anything, I felt exhilarated."

"Good for you," I said. As for myself, I was just hoping to survive lunch.

"But it's more than that. I've begun to feel that my body is changing inside this coat. That my lungs are getting stronger, that my limbs are becoming more powerful. In sum, that this coat is creating a new body for me."

"Look, Arthur, I don't believe anything about this story, it's preposterous. But if I did accept what you're telling me, I'd have to say that it sounds like you're taking a big risk here. You say that you can't

41

take the coat off. That suggests like you're trapped. Maybe that's what the coat was designed to do in the first place. Maybe that's what happened to its previous occupant. The coat swallowed him."

"Maybe it did. On the other hand, maybe it improved him. Maybe it released him back into our world as someone better and stronger than he had been."

"Why would it do that?" Arthur shrugged. "It's not hard to see that mankind is facing any number of threats to its existence: global warming, new pathogens, and nuclear war, among others. Isn't it possible that some alien race has decided to intercede to make sure that the human race survives, or, at least, some of us? Who knows what this coat will do for me? Maybe I'll be able to take more radiation than anyone else. Maybe I'll be immune to the next plague. Or, maybe it's just that I'll be one of them, one of the aliens, if they should come to this planet."

"I think you need help, Arthur."

Arthur misunderstood what I was saying. "I suppose I could go to a doctor and ask that he remove the coat. I suppose I could go to the government and tell them that I'm wearing an alien machine. But I suspect that whomever I tell would either conclude that I'd lost my mind, or would start running tests on the suit with, necessarily, me in it."

"What can I say?" Arthur sighed. "We're both coming to the end of our lives. Who wouldn't be willing to take a chance on something that might prolong his life, perhaps, even improve it? It might be that there's some new beauty in this transformation. It might be that it will allow me to see and understand better than ever before."

Neither of us spoke for a minute or two. That made me uncomfortable, so I tried to make a joke. "Well, I guess the aliens must have a sense of style to design their machines to look like trench coats."

Arthur waved his hand in front of his face. "Bryce, isn't it obvious why it looks like a trench coat? It's a disguise. No one has noticed me in this trench coat. It's allowed me to change into a new form while in plain view. For all I know, there're millions of us walking around. I mean, how many people have you seen in khaki-colored trench coats?"

That was enough for me. I proceeded to make it clear that I thought he needed psychological help, but he dismissed all of my concerns and, instead, muttered that he had been a fool to expect me, with my demonstrated lack of imagination, to be open to what was an extraordinary event.

We parted on such strained terms that I rushed up the street to console myself with some chicken in a curry sauce.

A few months later, the English Department hosted a cocktail party for a poet who had won an award for a book of poetry that consisted largely of punctuation marks and numbers. I wasn't surprised that Arthur was a "no-show," but I began to feel some concern when one of the professors mentioned to me that Arthur had been reported missing.

He explained that one of Arthur's relatives had arrived on an unannounced visit and had found the front door unlocked. When he walked in he found that Arthur's starving and frantic cat, Ezra, was in the process of wrecking the kitchen in order to get at the food in the cabinets. No one appeared to have been home for a week.

Of course, it was easy to conclude that poor Arthur, in the grip of his *idée fixe*, had wandered off somewhere, or had even done himself in. So far as I could tell, that's what the police assumed. It made it easier for them, I'm sure. I doubt that they had a place in their statistics for a disappearance associated with an alien coat.

I don't really know why I decided to stop into the vegetarian restaurant after the faculty party, but I was determined to make at least a small effort to locate my old colleague. The place wasn't crowded. This allowed the hostess to take a minute to speak with me about Arthur, whom she knew by name.

"I haven't seen him for a while," she said, "and I was hoping that he would come by because I think he left his coat here."

When I asked to see it she escorted me down a hallway to a small closet in the back of the restaurant. The only item in the closet was a khaki-colored, below the knee length trench coat with straps across the shoulders. There was neither an address, nor a manufacturer's label inside the coat, but I told the hostess that I recognized it as Arthur's.

"I'm sure that this belongs to him," I said. "I know where he lives and I'll be glad to drop it off at his house." She told me that I was welcome to take it.

Arthur's coat is hanging from a hook in my attic until such time as he returns. I can't say that I'm absolutely convinced that the thing is, as Arthur believed, an alien machine, but Arthur's disappearance has made that possibility real enough that I would prefer to keep the coat out of circulation.

At times I speculate about what might have happened to him, assuming that he didn't just wander away and end up in the local homeless shelter or psychiatric hospital. I would like to think that, whatever happened, he came to no harm.

Assuming that he was right and that the coat did transform him into some sort of genetically modified, hormonally improved superman I hope that he is enjoying his new existence either here, or on some other planet. Maybe he ended up with giant butterfly wings and just flew away.

But it's also possible that things just didn't work all that well. Maybe the aliens couldn't imagine everything that they would come up against on earth. I can picture a lab full of alien engineers saying something like, "Oh, now we see that rain shorts out the electrical system. We'll have to change that."

The fact that the coat showed up empty twice at the vegetarian restaurant suggests to me that the coat may have reacted badly to the something that was present there. I don't mean to imply that the food there was toxic, even though it may have tasted that way, but I remember a cousin of mine who had to be rushed to the hospital after eating some sesame noodles that were made with peanut butter. Maybe the suit was impervious to everything except what its occupant ingested.

I have considered trying the coat on. Arthur thought the benefits of the coat were worth whatever risk was involved. Whenever my knees ache from going up or down the stairs, my thoughts turn to the coat and its comforts.

But I remember that Arthur said that once he had put the coat on, he couldn't take it off. I have always avoided committing to acts that were irrevocable. I have to confess that Arthur was more the great Romantic hero than I.

Anyway, I haven't destroyed the coat because I have to wonder if, somehow, Arthur is still in there, even if I can't see him. I have a real fear that if I throw the coat into the incinerator, I will hear Arthur screaming as it burns. It may be that by keeping his coat around I've done more than keep just his memory alive.

Of course, I wonder if someday someone, perhaps in a khaki-colored trench coat, will drop by and ask for Arthur's coat back. I won't hesitate to give it up if that ever happens. It probably pays to stay on the good side of the aliens. Maybe they'll tell me when the apocalypse is due. I've booked a stay in Spain for next year, so I'm hoping to get that in before everything goes to hell.

A Transmission to the Home World

The first year of our emigration has gone well, praise Gleck. We have established our colony in the location designated as Bob and Edna's Trailer Park in Munsonville, in the "state" of Indiana, which is so named because "Indians" once lived here. "Indians" are now referred to as "Native Americans," so our expectation is that the "state" will soon be renamed "Native Americana."

Through the grace of Gleck, we have persevered, indeed, flourished in this wilderness so many light years from our own beautiful planet. Our community now numbers more than two hundred souls and we have already begun to plan an expansion into the nearby Coalburg Assisted Living Care Center where cable TV is available.

I regret to say that there have been losses among the faithful. I think particularly of young Unit AB 27673, who was called to sit at the heavenly console with Gleck after the human male Roy Sherman mistook his interest in questioning human female Tammy Mae Siddons as "coming on to her." We will long remember UB 27673 for his inquiring mind.

Fortunately, most of the data that he had collected on human sexual activity in places of public intoxication had been downloaded before Mr. Sherman acted on his threat to "bust a cap in your ass." We believe that the entry point was more likely the chest cavity.

Our holographic disguises continue to function adequately for the purpose of initiating and maintaining contact with the humans. Humans seem unable to recognize us as "aliens" although we understand that the agents of the government are constantly looking for us at various worksites.

However, our disguises have, on occasion, had unintended consequences for the user. In particular, due to our incomplete knowledge of gender identity in the cultural context of a human trailer park there have been several incidents of confused social interaction.

For example, Unit CX 34628 was given the holographic projection of a human female of approximately seventeen years of age. She was dressed according to the images that we had obtained from a computer scan of human print and electronic media.

We soon learned that her plaid miniskirt and white blouse tied to expose her midriff provoked an unexpected reaction among the human male population. She has since been issued a carbonizing weapon.

I, too, have had some difficulty maintaining my role as widow of a certain age living out a lonely existence with only the bitter-sweet memories of a past romantic relationship to sustain her. On several occasions, a human male of approximately thirty years of age who is known as "Vinny" approached me while I was planting flowers along the borders of my lot (the begonias are doing so well this year) and suggested that I would be well advised to "loan" him some value of currency.

Despite my repeated negative response, Vinny persisted in his entreaties. Furthermore, he began to intrude upon my personal space while proposing a series of ridiculous hypothetical questions, such as whether anyone would miss me if I happened to go on a permanent vacation and whether I would like to take a long ride from which I might not come back.

I was only able to convince "Vinny" to desist from these endeavors by altering my holographic appearance to that of a large Wrath Beast complete with tentacles and fanged suckers. "Vinny" was sufficiently unnerved by this transformation that he immediately removed himself from my presence and, in fact, from the trailer park, much to the disgust of Bob and Edna to whom he owed rent.

I'm sure it will amuse you to hear that the sight of a Wrath Beast is so daunting to the humans. As we both know, Wrath Beasts never attack. That is, unless they sense fear.

Despite the distractions caused by our interactions with the local human population, we continue to focus on honoring Gleck and his works, the very reason for our flight from the home world and our colonization of this planet. However, I note that our efforts in this regard have been hampered by our inability to find accommodations for the sacred ceremonies of Gleck worship.

As you might imagine, this can be a tough task. Just consider the amount of square feet necessary to allow us to set up the tubs of liquid nitrogen, the corundum tapestries and the steam table for the after-service buffet.

I concede that our initial efforts in obtaining a common area were somewhat misguided. We had received intelligence that humans often rented rooms for meetings in buildings established for community or charity purposes. We had also learned that one organization called the "AA" had leased space in virtually every village, town, and city in the "United States."

Therefore, we applied for the use of the basement of the local Baptist Church (they are *not* Gleck worshippers) under the name of the "AA." However, when two hundred of us appeared for our "meeting" it caused some comment from the pastor of the church despite our assurances that we were all "friends of Bill" and proud of it.

Since that incident, we have broken up into smaller study groups and have obtained space under the guise of being "clubs" of bridge players, bird watchers, and sex addicts. We hope that our occupation of the Coalburg Assisted Care Center with its large community room will allow us to meet once again as a unified congregation, praise Gleck, although we understand that the best hours of usage are often booked well ahead of time.

Our system for covert communications remains functioning and we have had no difficulty receiving messages from the home world through the broadcast of television programs. It appears that the humans are unaware that use of the phrase, "But I love you, Victor" during the "The Young and the Beautiful" indicates a sub-audio data transmission is in process.

Our inability to predict the specific time at which these transmissions will occur during the programming requires that we watch the entire show whenever it is broadcast (generally weekdays, 2:00 pm–3:00 pm CST), but we have heard few objections from the faithful due to the general interest in whether Lilly will recover from her amnesia and discover that Gregg, whom she believes is her long lost half-brother, is actually Drago, her ex-lover from Bolivia, who is intent upon seizing control of the Stanwood family's potash mines.

Plans for our future on this planet remain fluid. Those of us who are most intolerant of the indigenous population want to go ahead and drop the smallpox bombs already.

Others among us wish to proselytize for Gleck. They suggest that we set up trading posts and open commerce with the humans by offering them useful goods, such as cyborg drones, radiation proof alloy shielding and Vellapure (trademark registered) a meat substitute that is both nutritious and delicious.

In my own view, while the annihilation of all human life on this planet is arguably a bit too harsh, I wonder whether the simple minds of the humans would ever be able to grasp the subtleties of the doctrine of Gleck worship.

Would humans comprehend that it is Gleck's right eye that is all-seeing or would they fall too easily into the damnable Kadunian heresy that it is Gleck's left eye that is the source of his power?

Left eye, indeed! I curse those who would propagate such vile lies about Gleck. Of course, my dear friend, I know that you share with me a belief in the doctrine of dextral omnipotence, so, perhaps, I'm just preaching to the choir here.

As a compromise between these positions, I have suggested that we invite a small sub-group of humans to a celebratory dining experience, perhaps, after they have gathered in their crops for the fall.

My granddaughter, who is known here in the holographic disguise of "Gladys" a part-time school bus driver, has put together a document consisting of brightly colored pages depicting Gleck's destruction of the Voldrainians. It really is the cutest thing you will ever see.

I propose that we make this series of images available to the humans in a casual way, say by leaving it out on the coffee table, so that we can see whether they react favorably.

If they say that they want to learn more about the great and powerful Gleck, we can proceed further with a program of religious education. If they, instead, show indifference, or if they dishonor Gleck by placing beverages on his image and leaving awful stain marks, then smallpox bombs it is.

Obviously, I would like to hear your opinion on this great issue. If you would prefer to avoid the use of the TV transmission and submit your thoughts to me in private, please go to my Facebook timeline and annotate my last "life event" which is "I did not destroy the humans today" with an appropriate emoji.

Any-hoo, I won't be around for a while. I just picked up a flat of pink cosmos from Home Depot and I want to plant them interspersed among the begonias to create more of a tiered effect. I'll check the web when I get back.

Yours in Gleck,
Unit TD 34960

The Way of the World

The entrance to the bar was lit up like a movie premiere, but inside it was dim. The three heavy-set men who had wandered in from the parking lot blinked while their eyes adjusted to the darkness before taking seats at the only table in the place. A moment later, a teenage boy trailed in after them.

One of the men wrapped a muscular arm around the boy's waist and pulled him into a chair. "Sit down, kid," he ordered. "This is where the party starts."

The bartender had had his back to the entrance when the men entered. Now, he turned around and approached the men at the table.

"It's like a tomb in here," one of the men said. "Turn on the lights, would ya?"

The bartender shrugged. "The owner wants to save money." He spoke with an accent that Rick, the kid, thought was Hispanic. The bar was near enough to the border with Mexico for that to be a logical assumption.

"What's your pleasure, *senor*, beer, whisky, or tequila? That's all we serve." The bartender stood by the table while the men looked at each other.

The three men who had dragged Rick here were construction workers who had no trouble throwing around concrete blocks and rebar, but the bartender looked big enough to handle all three of them. Rick was praying that there wasn't going to be any trouble.

"Whisky," the man who had grabbed the boy replied. "We're celebrating a birthday. Bring us a bottle."

The men started razzing Rick while they waited for their drinks. "This is your 21st birthday, for God's sake," one of them said in a voice loud enough that the bartender could hear it. "This is your big chance to get laid. Why are you so scared? Do you want to stay a virgin forever?"

The bartender brought the bottle on a tray with four shot glasses. After he had put the tray on the table he lingered like he was expecting a question from the men.

One of the men shook Rick by the shoulder before he turned to the bartender. "So, *amigo*, we hear you've got some women here who might be looking for some companionship."

"In the back, three girls, twenty per fuck," the bartender said while he looked Rick full in the face.

The men laughed again, then reached into their pockets and took out their wallets. Two of the men threw twenties on the table. The third threw forty dollars on the table and said, "That's for the kid when he wants it."

The bartender didn't move. "It's another twenty for the whisky." he said, then added, "Leave by the back door, we don't want to attract the attention of the law."

"Sure, but if the kid doesn't use his fuck, I want my twenty back." The man threw another twenty on the table and strolled through the beaded curtain at the back of the room.

The other two men tossed down their drinks and stood up. One of them motioned "after you" to the boy, but he refused to get up from the table. He called back to Rick, "Okay, but you're only getting sloppy seconds."

The bartender gathered up the pile of bills and went back to the bar. He didn't ring the register.

Rick poured himself a glass of whisky. He drank it quickly and then poured another. After he had finished the second glass he walked over to the bar. He could feel that he was a little unsteady on his feet. He stood in front of the bartender and shouted, "It's a filthy business, what you're doing here."

The bartender put a glass on the bar top and poured whisky into it. He pushed the glass toward the boy. "Don't worry," he confided, "the girls like it."

"Oh, sure, they like being tied to a bed and being fucked all day. Who wouldn't?"

"Maybe they just like to have company."

"Fuck you," the boy said.

"They're very pretty, these girls, very hot. Men melt just looking in their pretty brown eyes."

"You're a cynical bastard, aren't you? Aren't you going to tell me they're all virgins, too?"

The bartender laughed. "Always have been and always will be." He wiped the bar with a rag. "Anyway, isn't that what everybody wants? Doesn't everybody want to be the first to corrupt that young sweet flesh?"

"No way," the boy shot back.

"Don't you want to be the strong one, the one who overcomes all resistance, the one who forces himself upon another's body giving it both pain and pleasure as you take what you need from it?"

Was it Rick's imagination, or had the bartender dropped his accent and hadn't his voice become more resonant and powerful?

"Don't you want to see that collapse, that *petite mort*, and afterwards, perhaps, the blood, the small red tear-shape on the bed sheet that proves your conquest?"

"What are you talking about? Is that supposed to be poetry?" Rick found himself breaking off eye contact from the bartender and stepping back from the bar.

The bartender cocked an ear toward the back room. "It sounds pretty quiet back there. Sounds like your friends were pretty quick. Here's a deal for you, you can have three for the price of one. Now, are you getting laid tonight, or not?"

"I'm just going to drive back to the construction camp by myself and leave these guys here. They can walk back for all I care."

"Your friends paid for you. Don't you want to have some fun. C'mon, virgin, aren't you going to get your cherry popped?"

"They're not my friends," Rick shouted. "They're just guys I work with. When they heard it was birthday they insisted I come to town with them for a drink. It was only after we got here that they started talking about getting laid. I guess they figured out I hadn't been with a woman before."

Rick finished the whisky and turned to leave, but the man at the bar grabbed him by the arm. "Stay," he said, "your friends will need you to drive them back. You owe them that, don't you."

"Not really, they're assholes," the boy said. He walked back to the table and sat down.

He knew that the guys who had brought him here would jeer about his refusal (they would call it a failure) to take advantage of the women. Tomorrow they would humiliate him in front of the other men. But he knew that it would be difficult for him at the camp if he didn't stay friends with them. He also had to admit that just because they were older than he was and because they knew more about the world than he did that the men had a certain fascination for him.

There was another part to his decision to stay, one that he found both confusing and embarrassing. Just the idea that a few steps away there were women who, voluntarily or not, were available to fulfill his physical desires filled his mind with sexual images. He couldn't stop himself from imagining the bodies of the women and how it would feel to touch their skin and lie upon their breasts.

"It's hard to walk away from that, isn't it?" the bartender asked. He seemed to have read the boy's mind. "Hear me out, kid. I'm just a small businessman myself. You know how we're always griping about government regulations, about how Uncle Sam is everywhere these days. I've got the same complaints, but it's a little different for me."

The bartender was polishing a glass, but the boy wondered how he would know if it was clean. The place was so dark. There wasn't even a mirror behind the bar.

"I remember when this part of the country was completely lawless. I don't just mean that there were *banditos* and drifters around. I mean that there just wasn't any law, period. No sheriffs, no chiefs of police, no FBI, just a few isolated military posts. If someone went missing, no one went looking for him because no one knew that he was missing. Now, everything's on the internet. Everything's on TV. If someone disappears, it's on the 10 o'clock news and there's a mob of volunteers out looking for him. It makes it hard for me and the girls to do business."

Rick was sure that the bartender was mocking him. "What are you talking about? What does that have to do with running a... well, a bordello?"

"We all have needs, kid. Me and the girls, we need things that aren't that easy to come by. So we have to keep low to the ground. Know how we do that?"

The bartender was staring at him so intently that the boy gulped. His mind was racing off in a different direction than sex.

"We stay hidden because it looks like we're just part of the same rotten system that everybody knows is out there, but nobody really wants to see. I can pay off the authorities because they think I'm just a flesh-peddler, just one of the scumbags that they've always done business with, no one to worry about. To them I'm just another entrepreneur in the world's oldest profession."

"As for the girls, well, no one is more invisible than the people you're exploiting. If you see them, you look away, maybe from shame, maybe because you don't want to care about what's happening to them, and, then, you try to forget that you ever saw them. But, kid, don't think we're selling anything here because what we're doing is taking. That's the way of the world."

The bartender must have thought that what he said was pretty funny because he opened his mouth like he was laughing. But what he opened wasn't really a mouth. It was more like a cave and it was a cave that was filled with stalactites and stalagmites, razor sharp and white and grooved like liquid had been running down them.

Rick fell off his chair. He just stayed on the floor, too frightened to get up.

All of a sudden, the bartender was a normal looking guy again. He said to the boy, "You'll find your friends outside in the back. They won't remember what happened. They'll feel weak. It'll be like they had too much to drink. Maybe they'll wake up tomorrow with a headache. Just get them into the car and drive them back to the camp. Tell them they must have had one hell of a good time.

Some of them may want to come back here. They may feel like they're drawn to something here. If they are, just let them go. Don't come back yourself because if you do, well, the girls are waiting and this time they may want more than just your cherry."

Rick backed out of the bar and ran around to the rear of the building. He found two of the men leaning against the wall next to the rear door and the third lying on the ground. He helped each of the men in turn to the car that they had borrowed from the construction company.

With his handkerchief he wiped away the small smears of blood on the men's throats. They slept while he sped back to the work site. There wasn't any traffic, but he kept checking his rearview mirror even though he wasn't sure what he was looking for.

The Good Life

Ms. Fay, our real estate agent, was an imposing woman. She was slender and walked with the straight back of one who had been trained as a dancer or model. She kept her grey hair up in a neat bun and wore simple, conservative dresses that probably cost a fortune. Whenever she wanted to emphasize some point about one of the houses she was showing us she would flash a brilliant smile that made you forget the laugh lines at the edges of her hazel eyes and the small creases in her neck.

"She must have been a beauty when she was young," I whispered to my wife, Julie, who gave me a look and whispered back, "Older women are beautiful, too. Don't be such a jerk."

I'm sure it would have branded me as even more of a jerk if I had wondered out loud just how much money it cost Ms. Fay to maintain her elegant look. Not only was she dressed well, but she wore several expensive pieces of jewelry that flashed red and green from her ears and fingers.

As she drove us around the countryside in her white Mercedes, I considered how many such women I had met through my job at the private bank. We only handle accounts of two million dollars or more. Most of our clients are businessmen who are sometimes accompanied by their wives, either fashionably appointed older women or younger women who wear short dresses and seem extremely bored with everything. And, of course, there are many blue-blooded widows who arrive at our offices in limos driven by men wearing chauffeur hats.

Unfortunately, my association with the rich has not helped make me rich. My family was of the type that describes itself as comfortably well off. My father was a lawyer and my mother was a teacher. They had been able to afford to send me to a good prep school and good liberal arts college. After I had graduated my father had used a few business contacts to help get me my present job, but my position there remained very junior and mostly involved the customer relations work that the partners didn't like to do.

I made a reasonably good salary, but it was only the inheritance that I had recently received from my mother's estate that made it possible for us to consider buying property in one of the old established suburbs. We had already agreed to the sale of our condo in the city, so we had to find someplace to live, but the rise and fall in value of our condo over the previous few years had made us a little wary about plowing our money back into real estate. Now we were in the hands of the formidable Ms. Fay who was showing us the stone and brick colonials that lined a wooded valley twenty miles north of the city.

Nothing appealed to us. If I liked a house, Julie found something objectionable about it. If Julie said that a house had possibilities, I said that it was a money pit. One place had a charming creek running beside it. My wife told me that it would flood. At last, after we had taken a break to sip lattes and eat sandwiches that came wrapped in cellophane, Ms. Fay announced that she had one more house to show us.

"It's in the town where I live. It's an estate sale and I think that it would be within your budget. I think that you might like it," she said and then added with a bright smile, "It even might like you."

On the drive over, Ms. Fay gave us some information. "It's an old farm house, mostly unrestored, but it has modern plumbing and electrical. I sold it to a gentleman about thirty years ago. He didn't live in it much. He was a writer and tended to travel. He didn't have a wife or any children. He died last year in Paris and the sale was held up while his administrator tried to locate all the possible heirs. But the

58

legal issues have been settled now and I have full authority to show the place."

Julie wanted to know the name of the previous owner.

"Well, I'm not sure if I'm supposed to tell anyone, but I'm assuming that you can keep a secret." Ms. Fay slowed down and turned her head toward my wife, "It was Walter Powers' house."

"Oh my god," Julie sputtered, "I didn't know he was still alive. Well, I mean that I didn't know he was still alive until last year."

I judged by my wife's reaction that Powers was someone I should know of, but I didn't recognize his name. As she so often did, Julie spotted my ignorance right away.

"He wrote a couple of books that were really big with the critics. They were very surrealistic and full of encounters with angels and weird beasts. Sort of Blakean. I heard that he did a lot of drugs."

Ms. Fay gave a throaty laugh, the first I'd heard from her that day, and said, "Well, I wouldn't know anything about that. I didn't know him very well. I only met him when I sold him the house. He was just out of graduate school then. He struck me as rather shy. He said he needed peace and quiet so he could write."

"He must have written those books here," Julie said, "but then he just sort of dropped off the literary map. I don't think anyone had heard from him for years."

"Yes," Ms. Fay responded. "He suddenly decided he had to go to Paris. He dropped everything and just ran off. I don't think he ever wrote anything worthwhile again. We were all so disappointed."

It seemed to me that this contradicted Ms. Fay's previous statement that she didn't know him at all, but I didn't say anything and, a moment later, we drove up a long driveway to a white two-story house set in a small clearing in the trees.

Both Julie and I were taken with the house as soon as we stepped in the front door.

"Look," Julie shouted, "built-in bookshelves."

"And a fireplace," I said.

The kitchen was large and modern. The closets were ample. There was a beautiful view of the woods from the upstairs bedrooms. We liked the bathrooms. We loved the floorplan.

But it was more than that. We both felt a sort of energy in the house. It sounds silly, but as soon as we had walked in we both seemed a little more awake, more aware, even a little more joyful.

Julie did a little dance in the upstairs hallway as we moved from room to room. When we came downstairs, Ms. Fay asked if we would like a little time to make up our minds. "No," I replied as I looked at Julie's shining face, "we've decided. We want to make an offer."

Ms. Fay took us back to her office to draw up the offer. She parked behind a townhouse and she walked us around to the street. "This is Saltonstall," she said. "This is Main Street and here's my shop. After you've signed the papers, I'll give you a chance to walk around and make yourself acquainted while I call the estate about your offer."

Inside, we sat in two leather wing chairs before an imposing dark wood desk while Ms. Fay went through her papers. I cleared my throat. "We haven't exactly discussed a monetary figure, Ms. Fay."

"Well," she replied, "You know what the asking price is."

Indeed, I did. It was well into the high six figures. I was wondering how low ball I could go when Ms. Fay interrupted my thoughts.

While giving me her most brilliant smile she named a figure just on the edge of the maximum that I had calculated we could afford. I looked at Julie. She shook her head up and down in enthusiastic agreement. I turned back to Ms. Fay and nodded.

"Perfect," she said and then read off the fees and taxes before concluding with, "I think I told you before I am familiar with the administrator representing the estate. I'm sure he'll be very receptive to the offer you've made. Now, why don't you stroll around our little town while I give him a call?"

I had had some hesitancy about the wisdom of committing to such an expensive house, but my doubts vanished as Julie and I walked around Saltonstall. It was such a perfect town.

We strolled past a hardware store, an apothecary shop, a florist's, a tea room and a boutique. There was not a Starbucks, a McDonalds, or a Dollar Store to be seen.

While Julie checked out the boutique I went into a store with a sign that said "The Spirit Shop, est. 1740." It was a bigger place that I had expected. I wandered down the aisles looking at the labels on the bottles and wondering how the heck even village wines from Burgundy had gotten so expensive.

As I had walked in, I had noticed a 60-ish man with a full head of grey hair and a salt and pepper goatee behind the counter. After a few minutes, he strolled over and introduced himself. He told me his name was Benjamin Firestone and that he was the owner of the store. He asked if he could help me find anything.

"No, thanks," I said. "I'm just looking around. My wife and I are thinking of buying a place here."

"Ah," he replied. "You must be working with Ms. Fay. I believe she has an exclusive on all the property inside the town limits."

"Yeah, we were just over at her office. We're making an offer on a place we saw today."

"Well, good luck. Everybody loves it here. I'd try to sell you some Dom to celebrate, but Ms. Fay always gives her clients a bottle when they move in."

I told Mr. Firestone that I would certainly be looking forward to that. I also said that I hoped to visit his store again if we moved into the area. "I've got to go, now, though. My wife's probably waiting for me."

He waved as I went through the door. "Next time you're here take a look at the Romanee in the back. I keep it temperature controlled."

Julie was outside in front of the boutique. "They had beautiful things," she said, "but nothing I can afford."

"Tell me. Everybody here is as rich as Croesus. The owner of the liquor store was wearing an Italian suit."

Julie shrugged. "It's going to be tough keeping up with the Jones's around here."

"The van Jones's," I said. "Maybe we'll be pals with Cornelius and Nelson. And isn't that stately Wayne manor down the road?"

Julie laughed and put her hand in mine. We turned and walked back to Ms. Fay's office where Ms. Fay informed us that our offer had been accepted and we were new land owners in Saltonstall.

"I hope you know how lucky you are." Ms. Fay said. "There hasn't been another property in Saltonstall to come up for sale since William Stellers' place hit the market last year,"

Later, as we were driving back to the city, Julie asked me if I knew who William Steller was. "Wasn't he the guy they caught selling electronics to the Chinese?" I replied. "I think he got 20 years in prison for that. He owned some sort of computer company that made secret stuff for the military."

"Oh," Julie said. She put her head against my shoulder and added, "I'm so glad we were able to get this house. I think it'll be perfect for us." Then she fell asleep.

On Monday, I sat in the office of my boss, Paine Rowden, and explained why I would need some time off during the next month. Paine has a large space at the back of the bank and among themselves the junior officers often referred to him as "Paine in the rear."

I didn't particularly like Paine, but I knew that he had the authority to fire me whenever he chose and Paine didn't particularly like me, but my work made his department look good, so we both made an effort to keep up an air of camaraderie. I always asked him about his golf scores and he always asked about the squash games I played at the Y.

I was telling him about the new house when he interrupted me. "Saltonstall," he muttered, "I've never heard of it. It must be really back in the boonies."

"The realtor told us it's been around since the late 17th century. She said it was founded by some group that came in from Massachusetts. They wanted religious freedom, or something like that.

It used to be called Old Scratchtown. The realtor said it was because everyone had to scratch for a living there."

Paine got to his point. "How are you going to get to work?"

I sighed. I could see Paine's mind racing ahead to the time when he would have the pleasant opportunity to reproach me for arriving late. "There's a train station about thirty minutes away. I'll have to leave earlier than I do now, but I'm sure I'll make it in before we open."

Paine's cell phone rang. He answered, but put the phone to his chest while he waved me away. "Sounds like a great place," he said. "Can't wait to see it at your Christmas party."

Every year I invited Paine to the Christmas party that Julie and I hosted. In nine years, Paine had never shown up once.

In early October, we went back to Ms. Fay's office for the closing. Ms. Fay was business-like and efficient as she walked us through the various forms. She had placed stick-on tags where we were expected to put our names. As the papers were handed over to us she would say, "Sign here and here and here."

I tried to make a joke to lighten things up. "I wish I'd taken more Latin in college. Then I might understand what I'm committing myself to."

Ms. Fay laughed. "There're very formal up here. If I hadn't done this so many times before, I might get confused myself."

At the end of it all, we had a deed to the property, title insurance, a receipt for taxes paid, and a mortgage from the local savings and loan. I had written a few checks and my inheritance was now a thing of the past.

After we shook hands with the loan officer and the attorney representing Powers' estate, Ms. Fay ushered us out of the conference room and back to her private office. As promised by Mr. Firestone, Ms. Fay presented us with a bottle of Dom Perignon. I offered to open it, but Ms. Fay declined. "Please," she said, "save it for a special occasion—just for the two of you."

Ms. Fay buzzed Felix, her personal assistant, who brought in tea and coffee with a tray of pastries. He also brought in a pot of herbal tea for Ms. Fay, who explained, "It's my own blend of herbal tea. I drink nothing else."

We snacked on the goodies and talked for a few minutes before Ms. Fay presented us with the keys to our new house along with a list of various contractors in the area. Ms. Fay assured us that these were good people and that we could rely on the quality of their work.

Just as we said our goodbyes and headed for the door Ms. Fay handed me one of her business cards. She had written a telephone number on the back.

"I'm sure you think that I'm being a busy body," she said, "but it can be hard to meet other people here. This is the telephone number of a client of mine who lives just a few miles from you. Give him a call. I'm sure he and his wife would love to have dinner with you. He's in the financial world, too, so I'm sure you'll hit it off. His name is August Kleinman. Have you ever met him?"

"No, sorry," I said and shook my head although I had met Mr. Kleinman once before and still remembered him all too well. Our meeting was not one that I liked to think about.

Why did I have the feeling that Ms. Fay already knew that?

About a year before we bought the house in Saltonstall I had gotten itchy and decided it was time to look for another job. Paine had always graded me well on my performance evaluations, but there was no indication that the higher-ups had any intention of moving me along to new responsibilities.

I had started sending out resumes. I was given some first interviews, but the only second interview I had been granted was with a hedge fund where August Kleinman was a principle.

Kleinman's secretary had called me at work and asked if I could meet Mr. Kleinman for lunch the next week. I agreed, of course, and the secretary gave me the name of an expensive steak house downtown where a few of the bank's customer liked to hang out.

"Mr. Kleinman will be there at noon," the secretary told me.

I had gone over Kleinman's bio before the meeting. He had been born in Austria, but, after his undergraduate work, he had moved to London where he had been a financial reporter for *The Economist*. A few years after that he had earned a master's degree in economics from Yale before moving on to Harvard Law where he had graduated at the top of his class. However, instead of practicing law, he had taken a job at the hedge fund where he'd been for about twenty years.

I did some research on the deals Kleinman was known to be involved in, prepared some questions that I thought would show how knowledgeable I was, and even rehearsed a few jokes in case he showed that he liked someone with a sense of humor. Of course, the lunch didn't go the way I had expected.

I had waited for Kleinman in a chair at the entrance of the restaurant. Well-dressed men and women had entered, taken a glance at me and passed into the dining area. It seemed to me that everyone was sizing me up and dismissing me. I was growing a bit frantic.

Just before one a short middle-aged man with a bulldog face – think Winston Churchill – entered and took my hand. "Ah," he said, "you must be Henry Chambers. I'm so glad to meet your acquaintance. Shall we ask for a table?"

Kleinman's diction was perfect, but there was more than a trace of a Germanic accent in his words. The *maître de'* came over immediately. "So good to see you, Mr. Kleinman. Will you be dining with us today?"

We were ushered to a table with what appeared to me to be more than the usual wait staff obsequiousness. Kleinman waved away the menu and ordered for both of us. "Two of your best Porterhouse, please, with spinach and creamed onions on the side and bring me a bottle of the Dominus from my cabinet downstairs." He did allow me to specify that I wanted my steak medium. He ordered his rare.

As we ate, I went through my spiel about how much I wanted to work for his firm and about how much I would bring to the job. Kleinman responded with a few polite questions, but for the most part remained silent.

We were midway through our steaks when Kleinman gave me look and said, "Mr. Chambers, I have read your resume. You have a good educational background and, so far as I can tell, you have a good reputation at the bank. You have good manners and you are well-spoken, but…." There was a distinct pause here. "But, Mr. Chambers, I do not think that anyone would call you a killer."

It took a few seconds for my mind to interpret what Kleinman had said, but when I understood what he meant, I had to agree. I wasn't particularly ambitious. I had never been the sort to put in eighteen hour days. I had never made much of an effort to cultivate my contacts with important people. Moreover, I wasn't the sort to make cold calls and sell securities to bewildered retirees. I didn't take dipsomaniac heiresses out for dinner and try to charm them into buying more of our financial products. I was a nice guy who did his job well. Until then, that had been all that I wanted.

We made polite conversation for the rest of the meal, but I already knew that I was out of my league with Kleinman. I knew that I was out of the running for the job even before the letter on beautiful stationary showed up. "Thank you," it said, "but we cannot offer you a position at this time."

In the weeks that followed the interview, I had gone over Kleinman's statement many times in my mind. At first, I had only been concerned with how Kleinman had decided I wasn't a "killer" and whether this was an opinion that people in the business generally held about me. But at some point, I began to wonder if Kleinman had meant to provoke me into revealing something more about myself. Maybe, he wanted me to say that I was a "killer." Maybe, he wanted me to say something that would change his mind and make him want to hire me.

It was around this time that I had started to see myself as something of a failure. There was certainly nothing about the experience that would make me ever want to face Kleinman again.

We moved into our new house in the middle of October. After a day unpacking our kitchen gear, Julie was ready to try to cook something in the oven. When I went up to shower, she left to go into Saltonstall. She said that there was a specialty butcher there and she wanted to pick up some nice chicken breasts for dinner. I expected her to be gone an hour, but she wasn't back for more like two.

I was watching TV when she came in. She brought in a bag from the butcher's shop and another bag with a wrapped object inside. She came over to where I was sitting and told me not to be mad at her.

"Why?" I asked. "Just because we're going to be eating at midnight?"

She punched my shoulder. "Don't be silly. I got back in plenty of time to make dinner. No, it's what's in the bag that I was talking about. I know things are sort of tight right now, but I just had to have that book. It's a first edition of *Linda Maestra!*, Walter Powers' second novel. The title comes from one of Goya's etchings. It was expensive, but I just thought it would be great to have it come home, so to speak."

Julie explained that while she was looking for the Butcher's shop she had found a real, honest to God, independent bookstore in Saltonstall. Of course, she'd had to go inside to see what sort of selection they had. She said it was a great place with piles of old books stacked up on tables and shelves that ran the length of the building.

"After a while," Julie said, "this distinguished-looking guy came out of the back and introduced himself. He told me his name was Robert Solpher and he'd owned the bookstore for years. I told him that we had just bought Powers' old place and he asked if I would be interested in seeing some firsts that Powers had signed for him. Well, I couldn't resist. So I bought this one. I hope you'll think of it as a house warming present."

I assured her that it was a great house warming present. She took the wrapping off the book and showed me the cover which had a picture of two witches, one young and the other old, flying on a broomstick. Inside the front cover there was an inscription from

Powers ("Bob, it's just been unbelievable!") and his signature with a date.

"This is such a great place," Julie said. "It's got everything." She took the book over to the built-ins. Julie hadn't unpacked her other books, yet, so this was the first book to go there. "That's the start of our Walter Powers collection," she exclaimed. "There's got to be other stuff around here about him."

I have to say that I always thought Julie was a little on the compulsive side. If she started a task she had to finish it no matter what. I guess that's what made her successful as a research librarian. Right now, I was wondering how much her interest in Walter Powers work was likely to cost us.

She walked back to the couch. "I know that there's got to be photographs of Powers all over Saltonstall. Solpher had one in his office. It showed Powers giving a reading, probably at Solpher's bookstore. I looked it over while he was wrapping up my book. Powers looked so young. And, you know, Solpher looked like he hadn't changed one bit."

Julie picked up the grocery bag and started toward the kitchen. She looked over her shoulder and said, "They must have great plastic surgeons in this town. Everybody looks so perfect. Maybe, I could find someone who could do something about my eyes."

I said, "Ms. Fay said that a lot of doctors lived in the area."

I wasn't looking forward to seeing Julie's credit card bill at the end of the month.

Everybody at work wanted to hear about the new house and I wasted the first morning I was back describing its charms. Around eleven, Jane, the receptionist, alerted me that Ms. Swenson was in the building. I had forgotten until then that she had made an appointment to see me.

If I say that I'm considered good-looking does that mean that I'm an egotist? I hope not. I wouldn't say I'm Hollywood handsome, but I have a strong jaw and high cheekbones and I always was given the lead role when I was in plays at college. I think that this is the reason the widows and even some of the wives who do business with the bank gravitate to me.

I don't know if Ms. Swenson had a crush on me, but she always asked for me when she had some financial matter that she needed taken care of. Now, she wanted to arrange a line of credit. It wasn't anything that I expected to take more than fifteen minutes.

Ms. Swenson was one of the old guard. She was the daughter of a railroad executive who had expected nothing more from her than that she make some promising young man a good wife. She had been given piano and drawing lessons, had attended one of the Seven Sisters' colleges, and had been allowed a grand tour of Europe before being married off to the son of the owner of a prosperous chemical concern.

She'd had what most people would consider to be a happy life. Other than giving birth to a couple of potential heirs, her marriage had consisted of arranging parties, directing a squad of domestic employees, and appearing gracious. Once her children had reached adulthood and her husband had passed away from a cancer possibly related to chemical exposure, she found herself with little to do. Her one remaining interest was in preserving the various gardens that she had developed around her house. It had become almost an obsession with her. And it cost big bucks.

Of course, Ms. Swenson had the money to support her hobby. It's just that it was tied up in various annuities and trusts and not easily accessible. That's why she wanted the line of credit. I wasn't sure what her new project was, but I think that it had something to do with saving the Monarch butterfly.

Ms. Swenson had dressed in a blue dress with a white collar and she was wearing a string of pearls and a garden hat. As she entered my office, I was struck by her resemblance to one of the mannequins Julie and I recently had seen in the costume section of the local museum. I could image her arranged on a pedestal with a label that said something like "Oscar de la Renta–1976."

"Oh, Mr. Chambers," she said with the sort of nervousness that I didn't associate with multi-millionaires, "I'm so glad you could see me. I hope that your bank is willing to advance the funds that I requested. What I'm doing with my gardens will be of paramount importance to saving a glorious species from extinction."

The bank had already decided to grant her the credit. There was no reason that we shouldn't. But I wanted Ms. Swenson to think that I had some authority in these matters, so I said in a voice that I meant to be stern although not harsh, "Certainly, Ms. Swenson, however, the bank must consider your long-standing financial interests before making such a decision. We wouldn't want to act precipitously."

I almost laughed when I said this because, after all, what Ms. Swenson was asking us to do was to lend her money that was already hers at a high rate of interest.

Ms. Swenson collapsed into one of the fake Queen Anne chairs in front of my faux Georgian desk and allowed me to pour her a cup of Lipton tea from the silver-plated tea pot that the receptionist had left on my desk when she had showed Ms. Swenson in.

After a few sips of tea, she seemed to compose herself. She leaned closer to me and, speaking in a tone that would be described in a stage direction as "confidential," she told me that she had some information to share about her personal worth that might affect my decision.

"As you know," she said, "my son has been running the company since his father passed away. Now, he expressly told me not to tell anyone about this, but his company is being acquired next month by DuPont. He says that I can expect the value of my stock to double when the deal goes through. So, as you can understand, I should be in very good position to pay off any debt I incur in re-building my native plant garden."

I held up my hand. "Please, Ms. Swenson. It's not necessary that I know these particulars. I think that your son was correct to tell you not to pass along such information. In fact, Ms. Swenson, I suggest very strongly that you not tell your son that we had this conversation. I'm sure that he would be quite upset and rightly so if he knew that you had mentioned the sale of his company to me."

I wiped my hand across my forehead. "Also, the bank has decided to grant your request for a line of credit. I have some papers for you to sign."

Before I went out to lunch I stopped by Paine's office. "Did you have any problems dealing with that old bird?" he asked.

"None at all," I said.

I was restless after lunch and asked Paine for the rest of the day off. He told me to go ahead and take care of anything I had to do for the new house. My guess was that as soon as I left he would make write down the date somewhere and make a note that I had left early for the day.

I called Julie while I was waiting for the train. When I said that I was on my way home she asked me to pick up some things that she'd left at the tailor's shop. She told me not to wait for her for dinner.

"Busy?" I asked.

"Busy," she said and hung up.

I managed to make it to Saltonstall by four-thirty. I parked on High Street and found the tailor's shop without too much trouble. Ms. Charbon, a trim forty-ish brunette in a grey skirt and white blouse was behind the counter.

I had introduced myself and we made small talk for a few minutes before she handed me a couple of skirts and a pair of slacks on hangers. Ms. Charbon added, "Tell your wife that I'd be happy to make that suit she was interested in, but she'll have to come back for me to get her measurements."

I walked back to my car with Julie's clothes slung over my shoulder. As I passed store window after store window decorated with black cats and pumpkins, I thought to myself, *Saltonstall really must love Halloween.*

The town had a clean, perfect look. There was nothing about it that suggested disorder. The streets were free of litter and the town square was pristine. Every storefront was filled with displays for expensive goods. In fact, it now occurred to me, the town was entirely devoted to shopping. On my visits to Saltonstall, I had never encountered anything like a factory, a warehouse, an apartment building, or a gas station.

And the range of businesses in the town was little strange, too. For example, there was a liquor store in town, but there wasn't a bar. There was a bakery, a butcher's shop, a greengrocer, and even a catering business, but no restaurant.

Really, the place seemed to close up after dark. After six in the evening every store was shut. It was as if the merchants had decided that they would be happy to sell you whatever you wanted during the day, but that they didn't want you to bother them at night. I wondered if there was a town ordinance that kept them from staying open longer, but I had to concede that the merchants seemed to do pretty well as it was.

It struck me that the merchants might really be better off than the nouveau riche who patronized their establishments. It seemed like every day some Wall Street financier racked up millions in losses backing the wrong stock. And then there was the wear and tear of life in the fast lane. Just today, I'd read in the paper about another rock star dying in a hotel room of an overdose of pain pills.

Of course, I knew nothing about the people who owned the stores. The signs on the stores said "est. 1740" or whatever, and who knew how many generations of families had come through Saltonstall. But, it seemed like the perfect symbiosis. The merchants created a place where the rich would want to live and the rich spent their money on what the merchants sold them.

I reached my car and while I was stowing Julie's clothes in the trunk I caught a glimpse of Ms. Fay in the tea room across the street. She waved at me to come over and, in an effort to show neighborliness, I locked the car and joined her.

Aside from Ms. Fay the only other person in the tea room was a petite young woman in a waitress uniform who was washing dishes at the sink. Ms. Fay motioned for me sit beside her and called out to the young woman, "Mary, would you bring Mr. Chambers a cup of coffee." Ms. Fay was drinking more of her herbal tea.

"I'm amazed," I whispered to Ms. Fay, "I thought those uniforms had gone the way of the Edsel and disco music."

She smiled at me and said, "But doesn't Mary look cute in it."

Mary did indeed look cute in it. She had a snub nose and freckles and looked like the cover girl for some product that promised to take away your acne. When she brought over my coffee, Ms. Fay said to her, "I know it's past your closing time, dear, but do you mind if we stay for a few more minutes?"

Mary assured us that she didn't mind and went back to do some more clean up behind the counter.

Ms. Fay turned back to me. "Mary was in college when she first found Saltonstall. She decided she wanted to stay and I was able to find her some people to live with." She took another sip from her tea cup and then said in a conversational tone of voice, "Do you know what Mary's favorite thing to do in the world is, Mr. Chambers? She likes to fuck rock stars. Whenever some band she likes come to the city I find out where they've got reservations and she goes there and fucks whomever she likes. I understand that Ms. Charbon has made her some really sexy outfits that show off her nice little tits and that bubble ass. Those rock guys can't believe their good luck when she pulls down their jeans."

I was horrified that Ms. Fay would say something so vulgar and outrageous. And, my God, that girl, Mary, was standing only about eight feet away. She must have heard every word. I tried to turn my head to see if she was still there, but I couldn't move.

The town had come to a stop. I felt my chair moving forward as the room grew bigger. The dusky light rose in a green and golden wave and fell through the window behind Ms. Fay. Her grey hair untied itself from its tight bun. She shook it out into giant blonde ringlets. Her eyes glowed like the moon behind high clouds. I wanted to look away. I didn't want to look away.

"Don't be scared of us," I heard her say in a low and seductive voice. "Don't run away like Walter. He thought he could be successful without us. He spent twenty years in a garret drinking himself to death. Work with us, Henry. Listen to what we say. We'll help you get rich. We can show you how to get everything you've ever wanted."

I felt myself filled with an emotion that I can only describe as an overwhelming desire, both for Ms. Fay, physically, and for everything I had never had in the world.

There was a pause. The tea room returned to its normal size and shape. I could see cars moving along the streets. Ms. Fay was standing. She'd left a twenty on the table.

She glanced toward me and smiled. "You might want to wait a little while before you stand up, Henry. I don't think Mary would be shocked, but she might laugh."

About five minutes later, I walked back to my car and drove home.

Julie's car wasn't in the driveway and no one answered when I shouted, "Anyone here?" from the front door. I went to the bar and poured myself two shots of bourbon, then went upstairs and searched my desk for the business card Ms. Fay had given me. When I found the card I dialed, Mr. Kleinman and introduced myself.

He was rather put out that I had his private number. He interrupted my introduction to demand how I had gotten it, but calmed down when I said that Ms. Fay had suggested that I call him.

"Well, what's this all about, Mr. Chambers? I'm sure my firm sent you a letter. We decided to hire someone else."

I said that wasn't why I was calling. I told him that I had certain information that I'd like to share with him although I didn't want to do it over the phone. I promised him that I wouldn't be wasting his time if he would consent to see me. I also said that speed was of the essence.

I guess he'd had similar dealings before. He said that he'd be available if I wanted to come over tomorrow night around eight. He gave me his address, said, "Good night" and hung up.

I made myself another drink and turned on the TV. There wasn't anything on that interested me and after an hour or so I decided to turn in. I don't know when Julie got home. I woke when she slid into our bed, but I went right out a moment later.

When Julie and I had lived in the city we had gotten up at the same time, had eaten breakfast together, and kissed each other good bye before we walked off to our jobs. We often would meet for lunch and sometimes would even hook up at our condo for what Julie would call "quickies."

After only a couple of weeks of living in the suburbs we were driving separate cars to the train station and taking different trains to work. I suppose it had to be that way. If we shared the drive to and from the station each of us would have had to accommodate the other's schedule. Neither of us wanted to hang around the city if the other had to work late or attend a business-related dinner.

The next morning Julie was taking her shower when I finished the last of my coffee and wrote her a note explaining that I would be meeting someone after dinner for drinks. I added, unnecessarily I suppose, that I would see her when I got home. I took a look in the hallway mirror, straightened my tie and set off for work.

Julie called me after lunch to say that she had seen my note and that she had something to do at the office that evening so she would be home late, too. She was only on the phone for a minute or two before she whispered, "I might have some interesting news for you tonight," and hung up.

I thought that I might have some interesting news tonight as well, but I wasn't sure that I was going to tell Julie about it.

I drove straight from the station to Kleinman's house which was a boxy, internationalist sort of building with a lot of windows. It looked entirely artificial although it was set incongruously, I thought, on a wooded lot landscaped with shrubbery the size of buses.

There was a steep driveway up to the house and I wondered how Kleinman was able to use it during the winter. Maybe he had a professional drive him to work every day.

A tiny woman with a widow's hump opened the front door and took me to see Kleinman. I thought at first that she might be Kleinman's wife, but I changed my opinion when he dismissed her with a curt, "Thank you, Gloria, I won't be needing you again, tonight."

Kleinman directed me to a leather chair next to a small table where someone had put out a decanter of red wine. "Have some, Mr. Chambers. It's a very fine vintage port. Mr. Firestone sent it over. He always saves his best for me."

As I poured myself a glass, Kleinman shouted upstairs, "Honey, I have a guest. Don't worry about coming down. We're talking business." Whoever was upstairs shouted back, "Sure. Whatever."

I assumed that this was the voice of the glamorous-looking women who stood next to Kleinman in a series of photos set out on the fireplace mantel. He always wore the same tux. In each picture she had a different gown.

Kleinman sat in a chair on the other side of the table. He poured himself some of the port and said, "So, Mr. Chambers, what's this all about."

I was pretty direct with him. I told him what I knew about DuPont buying the Swenson's chemical company and how I'd heard about it. I said that my information could make him a few million and that I wanted a percentage.

I knew that Kleinman might make money on the news I'd given him without giving me a cent, but I didn't think that he would. First, all I had done at this point was to pass a rumor along to friend. If Kleinman didn't cut me in I could rat him out to the SEC and he would be the one who had to kick back his profits and maybe lose his license. Second, if I could come up with this sort of information on this occasion who knew what other favors I might be able to do for him. I still had a lot of old birds to pluck.

We talked about the details of the deal for about thirty minutes. Kleinman would have a friend set up an account in my name at the friend's firm. Kleinman would purchase as much of the Swenson stock as he could without tipping the SEC or anyone else off. When DuPont disclosed that it had purchased the Swenson's company and the value of the Swenson stock shot up he would deposit a portion of what he'd made in my new account. We didn't bother to shake hands over it.

Kleinman walked me to his front door. "Perhaps, I was wrong about you, Mr. Chambers," he said as he ushered me out.

"Perhaps, you were," I said to myself as I eased my car down the slope of his drive.

I found Julie sitting at the dining room table. She had just tossed back a flute of champagne. "I opened the Dom," she said. "Why don't you have some?"

On the table in front of her I could see about thirty pages of stationary. I could see that the top page had Walter Powers' name embossed on it. The sheet was covered with lines of cursive writing in blue ink. "What's that?" I asked Julie.

"That," she said, "is an unknown short story, really a novella, written by the late Walter Powers in his own cramped handwriting."

I was alarmed. "You didn't buy that, did you?"

"No, my dear," she answered, "I found it."

"Where did you find it?"

"At the library."

"Well, did you tell them about it? I mean, isn't it theirs?"

"It all depends on how you look at it," she said and picked up the manuscript.

"Before Walter left for Europe he gave his papers to the library. He left so quickly that I'm not even sure that he signed the documents we usually require before we take a gift like this. Anyway, the library keeps his stuff back in the rare books room. It's a mess in there."

I poured Julie some more champagne before she continued.

"Walter gave us the drafts of his two novels, some personal effects, and his copies of the literary magazines that had published his early work. We didn't really need the magazines. We already had those, so they put them in a box and shoved them under a shelf. I'm so glad they never got around to deaccessioning them.

"I got interested in Walter when we bought the house and I thought it would be fun to look at the stuff the library had of his. The drafts and some of the other things, letters and such, are kept in a temperature controlled area under lock and key. I'm authorized to go in there so I had the chance to look them over. That was fun. Then I found a computer record about the magazines and I thought why not see what they were like, too."

She held up the manuscript. "This was folded up inside one of the magazines. The library didn't have a clue that they had it."

"Didn't somebody have to check Walter's stuff when it came in?"

"Sure and that's the good part." Julie put the manuscript back down on the table. "Not only did somebody miss the boat on the manuscript, but when the library transferred its written records to computer storage about ten years ago the only entry they put in about the box is something like 'twenty-two literary reviews belonging to Walter Powers.'"

"Babe," she said, "don't you see? We can sell this. Powers never won the Nobel or anything like that, but he still has a following and anyone who collects his stuff would pay a fortune for an unpublished, never-before-seen work of his."

Julie added, "And it's good, too. I've only skimmed it, but it has all the hallucinogenic imagery that he's known for. It fits perfectly into the canon. It's sort of a parody of Hawthorne's *Young Goodman Brown.* The narrative voice goes into the woods and sees his neighbors in some sort of witches' Sabbath thing, but he's not disgusted. He joins right in. He's pretty explicit about what goes on."

"Can't they trace that thing back to you?"

"No way. I mean, somebody might suspect, but how are they going to prove it? The library couldn't even prove that they had the manuscript to begin with. Anyway, nobody has to know that we're the ones selling it. Solpher will sell it privately for us. And if any serious buyer wants to look into the provenance of the manuscript, we've got the perfect story. We found it! We moved into Walter's old house and it was up in the attic or something."

"How about his estate?"

"Screw them," Julie shouted. "Look at our deed. They sold the place to us 'as is.' Whatever Walter left behind is ours now. Anyway, Walter didn't leave any heirs. Assume that there's an article in the *Times* that says someone bought the manuscript. Who's going to be around to complain?"

I tilted my flute toward Julie. "Finders keepers," I said.

Julie clinked her flute against mine. "Losers weepers." She drained her champagne and looked around the house. "Oh," she said. "I just know we're going to love it here."

I Just Have a Few Comments

Corey, Melinda, and I formed the core of the Wednesday Science Fiction Writing Group. Other people had drifted through in the two years we'd been meeting, but none of them had stayed for more than a few months.

We tried to make new people feel comfortable, but I can't say that I missed any of the writers who had come and gone. In particular, I didn't miss the woman whose name I have forgotten who submitted stories about a fantasy kingdom set in the Amazon where a beautiful queen ruled autocratically over a complaisant population and used her mystical powers against an army of rebel frogs.

She seemed to identify with the queen. Everyone else in the writers' group sympathized with the rebel frogs. Her stories were filled with misspellings and grammatical mistakes. When Corey suggested that her kingdom was, well, undemocratic, she snapped back that he obviously had no respect for "quality." We were all relieved when she stopped coming.

In truth, I thought that the group worked best with just of the three of us present. We knew each other's work and, more importantly, we respected each other's criticism.

In response to some of Corey's comments, for example, I had made several changes to the narrative thread of "The Quartzar Wars," my novel about a conflict between two kingdoms over a source of crystals that could power a star ship. And I knew that Corey had changed the gender of several of his "Cybernautic Warriors" after

Melinda had complained that he had no powerful female characters in his stories.

So, I tried to stay positive when Jed appeared for one of our meetings. Although he had introduced himself ahead of time by sending me an e-mail. I hadn't really expected him to show up. He had said that he hadn't put together anything in the way of a story, but he hoped that the writers' group would "inspire" him to start writing.

Can I say that Jed looked like a Mormon missionary? He was wearing a brown suit, a white shirt and a thin, red tie. He was pasty-faced and earnest. Whenever he spoke he leaned toward the person he was speaking to and talked directly into his face.

I had e-mailed everyone's work to Jed. As he took our stories from his book bag and sorted them into three neat stacks on the library table I could see he had marked each page in red ink with a complex series of symbols. They looked like what you might get back from an over-zealous teacher after you had failed a test.

I thought, I bet this is going to be good. Then, out loud, I noted that we were going to be discussing Melinda's story, "Cat Twirls," first.

Melinda was sort of a Goth girl. She painted her nails black and she wore lots of black mascara. She always showed up for our meetings in some sort of dark clothing. She wore a black beret that she never took off, even when she was inside. I think that her hair was naturally dark, but she kept it dyed in various pastel tones.

Corey and I were happy that she had joined the group. Corey and I had been friends since college and we spent a lot of time together, so having a third person made it seem more like a real writers' group and not just like the two of us carrying on with our usual conversations.

I opened the discussion about Melinda's story by saying that I liked how the cat turned out to be a time traveler and I also liked how the cat interacted with Margareta, the protagonist of the story. Corey said that he thought that Melinda had really done a good job setting out the "physicality" of the land of the giants and that he thought that it was really funny that Melinda had described the metal hats that the giants' wore as looking like Eifel Towers.

When Corey paused, Jed jumped in to the discussion by saying that he just had a few comments about the story. First off, he didn't understand how a cat could talk. "Felis catus," he told us, "does not have vocal cords that would be capable of producing human speech. Also, because of the ossification of the hyoid bone they can purr, but they cannot roar, as your cat does when he assaults the giant sentry."

He was also not too happy with the giants. "You describe the giants as humanoid in appearance, but a fifty foot humanoid would be structurally incapable of walking. A femur, even if proportionate in size to a fifty-foot human, would collapse when subjected to the stress of supporting that sort of weight."

"Dinosaurs get that big," I said.

"A dinosaur thigh bone," Jed replied, "is thicker and more robust than a human thigh bone. Dinosaurs evolved to be big. Humans evolved to be small."

"It's a fantasy," Melinda said.

"Yes, yes," said Jed, "that's why it should be correct in every detail."

That's pretty much how things went with each of our stories.

I thought that Corey was really onto something with his novel about "Cybernauts" who were able to enter and control computer networks while battling an evil dictator who controlled a future earth.

Jed launched into a long discussion about "gates" and "logic systems" that I didn't really understand, but it was obvious that he thought that electrical impulses from a human brain, even if directly downloaded into a computer network, would not have any influence on the actual processing performed by the network.

When my chapter came up for discussion I expected that Jed would have something negative to say about my description of the Kirilian star ships, but, instead, he focused on the "chain of command."

"Why would an admiral of the Kirilian Fleet wish to lead a mission to sabotage an enemy battle cruiser? One of such high rank would surely be more concerned with questions of strategy and logistics than with leading a squad of space commandos into battle. Would you expect one of earth's great generals, a George Patton, for example, to jump into a tank and say, 'Let's drive to Berlin and capture Hitler?'"

Jed seemed to like his own joke because, at this point, he broke into a series of high-pitched squeaks.

I snapped back, "Admiral DeBargian is a risk taker and an adventurer. He wants to be directly involved in any mission his men undertake. Also, it would be really dull if he just sat at a desk and issued orders."

"This Admiral," Jed replied, "would undoubtedly face a board of inquiry and be stripped of his rank and, perhaps, be sentenced to permanent sleep."

Everyone was quiet for a few moments. I noticed that Corey and Melinda hadn't bothered to say what, if anything, they liked about my story. I wasn't sure if they were cowed by Jed's criticism, or whether they were just giving him the silent treatment.

Jed seemed to recognize that the meeting had ended. He stood up and said, "I will certainly be glad to attend the next meeting of your Writers' Group. Goodbye."

After he had left, Corey asked, "What are we going to do about that guy? Do you think he's autistic?"

Melinda declared, "I'm not coming back if he's going to be here. I'm willing to listen to criticism, but that guy is a sadist."

I picked up my writing pad. "This group has always been pretty informal, but now I think we need to have a set of rules. I suggest that we try to define the parameters of how members should offer criticism."

Corey said, "I think we should just change the date of our next meeting and not tell Jed."

On his way back to his life pod, Jed considered what he should put in his report to Central Command. He had been charged with the mission of interacting with humans in order to assess their capacity for creative thinking.

If Jed determined that humans were imaginative enough to survive contact with an alien civilization the Command would initiate negotiations. Before he could recommend such a course of action, Jed wanted to be sure that humans could modify their mental constructs and paradigms without creating a destructive cognitive dissonance.

No one wanted a repeat of the Kodar situation where the entire planet had descended into chaos after a fleet of star ships had appeared over their cities. The Command had had no choice but to put the whole system under quarantine. There seemed to be no way other way to stop the witch hunts, the persecution of aliens, and the other hideous practices that the Kodarians had fallen into.

Right now, Jed was leaning toward "thumbs down" for the humans, but he did want to give them another chance. He had translated a portion of the "Grangrun," an ancient text that was full of paradoxes and mind-bending logic. He would read it at the next Writers' Group meeting.

Either it would open them to new ideas or it would drive them mad. Jed figured it was about 50-50 which way it went.

We've Only Just Begun

God, I hate that freaking Karen Carpenter. Her and that freaking song. Two verses. Like an infinite loop.

Yeah, I want another drink. Yeah, put it on my tab. Thanks. Now, why don't you go back to the bar? Find something to do back there and leave me alone. Maybe you could invent something. Ha, ha. I used to invent things. I used to be one of the smartest men in the world.

Christ, let me think for a second. Better still, let me stop thinking. Please.

How'd I end up with Karen Carpenter, for Christ sake? I never listened to that crap. I listened to Bud and Monk and Bird and Lovano and sometimes Mo…Mozart. Just goes to show what crap is floating around in your head, even in my head.

So, anyway, I used to be pretty smart. That's why they came to me. The government, I mean. They wanted something that would in…in…capitate. Not kill, they didn't want that. Kill was in…humane, just confuse, immobilize the suckers.

President probably directed them to do it. Not Obama. The guy who came after him. What was his name? You know.

Anyway, that was what they wanted us to do. Someone else was doing lasers. Someone else was doing viruses. Blah, blah.

I worked in the research lab for a biotech. I did sono…sono…sonogenetics. You know, I used sound waves to manip…change the nervous system.

Memories. That's what I was working on. Stimulate the brain! Smack the right neuron with the right sound wave and you can release an old memory. Get back all those memories you lost. All sort of medical uses. Non-invasive. Helps people with Alzheimer's. Good stuff.

But some genius at corporate HQ said we should weaponize it.

What's so bad about memories, you say? Well, Mr. Taxpayer, what if you have too many memories? Mass confusion.

If you stim…late as many memories as possible suddenly your head is full of the stuff you haven't thought about in years. All that stuff that brain housekeeping has swept under the rug comes back in a rush—what you were doing in the third grade in Ms. Munster's class and every dinner you've ever had and all those conversations you had with relatives who've been dead for twenty years.

That would screw everybody up good, wouldn't it? Everybody would go bonkers. So what? I didn't care. Labs run on money. M-O-N-N-E-Y! A kiss for luck and we're on our way, eh, Karen, you freaking bitch.

Anyway, so we needed a pulse, beam, something we could use to direct the sound. I mean, you couldn't put a whole army in something like a dentist's chair and just say sit quiet while I put this machine on your head.

Had to bring in engineers. That's where it went wrong. Engineers love failure. They love to quote Edison. Once you get them involved you know something's gonna go wrong. Workin' together day to day. Ha, ha.

So they built me a chamber. Someplace I could practice on chimps. First I'd zap 'em, then I'd monitor the changes in their brains.

Some grad student type brings in a chimp. Ties him down. No, no, I say. His head's not re…re…trained. I go in. I come out.

Engineer says, oh, oh, looks like we had a discharge while you were in there. How ya feeling?

Wha, I say. Who turned on the freaking Carpenters?

Cut to the chase. I've been hearing this one freaking song for weeks. It's like hearing elevator music. Except it's just one song. And the doors never open.

Alcohol helps. Calms me down. But I know I'm going crazy.

Freaking engineers. How'd you like to hear Karen Carpenter any time, all the time?

Been thinking I might go back to the lab. Do a little tinkering. Make a few changes. Next time those engineers flip on the switches it's Karen Carpenter time. Or maybe it's the Macarena. *Ole!* That'd really be hell.

Or maybe make it the big broadcast. Never figured out the range of our equipment, but I bet I could take out everybody in the building. Hello, Cost Accounting, it's time for some "We Built This City." How'd you like to hear that forever?

Gimme another bourbon! Now!

Maybe, you're right, Karen, so many roads to choose.

And we've only just begun.

Fear

Deputy Sheriff Ames had just pulled back the scrub when we all heard a sound like a rattle being shaken. *Snake* was my first thought and it was probably Ames' too. He already had his pistol drawn and he might have started shooting, but Chuck shouted, "Take it easy. It's just a bug."

It's strange, I suppose, that it was the sound that scared us and not the eight bodies.

We moved in to take a better look and spotted the thing crawling back and forth across the remains of the men. It looked like a hornet, but it was as big as a deck of cards. It had a yellow body and a tangerine colored head with giant mandibles.

Every few seconds, it would come to a stop and vibrate its wings. We figured that's what was making the sound. It looked like we had riled it up.

"Ever seen one of those things?" someone asked. We were all agreed we hadn't. This touched off a debate about what it actually was. Some of us thought it was some sort of hornet and some said it was a big bee.

"Well, whatever it is," Dawson said. "I'm not going to give it a chance to take a piece off of me." Dawson swung his shovel at the bug, but it was gone before the blade hit the bones. We ducked as it flew past us.

Ames was mad. "Shit, Dawson, you just messed up a crime scene. I could arrest you for obstructing justice." We all knew that the Deputy was scared of the Sheriff who had a reputation for being a tough SOB. The Deputy didn't want any sort of screw-up while he was on duty.

Chuck tried to smooth things over. "Look, there isn't anything particularly mysterious about what went on here. Some Mexicans came over the border and got caught in the desert without any food and water. God rest their souls."

"Oh, yeah," Ames shot back. "So tell me why we're looking at nothing much more than skeletons in clothes. Somebody saw these guys alive a week ago. Animals would have left more than we're seeing here. What happened to these guys?"

Up until then, I hadn't been thinking much about the cause of death. I'm a fireman and an EMT. I was there to try to save lives. I had brought water and an aid kit in my truck. For the worst case scenario I had brought body bags, but I hadn't expected to find that there was so little left of the dead.

We had come searching for the men after a rancher had reported them crossing his property. He had said that some of them looked ill and had to be helped along by the others. The Border Patrol had asked the Sheriff for help and he'd sent us. Ames and the other men carried rifles, but, considering the heat and the desert terrain they were walking through, we had expected that we were looking for men who were near death or already dead.

Ames continued throwing questions at Chuck. "And why the heck did they dig a hole in the ground and cover themselves up? It's a hundred degrees plus out here. Were they looking for some shade? They sure didn't think that one out real well."

I assumed that the deputy was being "rhetorical." Nobody knew what had really happened here. When none of us offered any answers, Ames walked back to his jeep to radio the Border Patrol.

While he was gone, Dawson and J. T. got into it with Chuck over the "illegals." Dawson and J. T. were of the opinion that anyone who tried to sneak across the border was "just asking for it." They seemed to think that the dead men had deserved to die of thirst and exhaustion.

Chuck was taking a more compassionate route saying that no one should have to die that way. It was up to the law to round illegals up and return them to their country. That's all people should worry about. He didn't hold it against the Mexicans that they wanted to get into America. It was the same sort of argument I'd heard too often over the last year.

I turned away from the other men and looked out at the Sonoran Desert. Patches of creosote covered the valley floor. In the distance a couple of saguaro stood upright with their limbs bending toward the sky like they were offering a greeting. Heat shimmered off the fine white sand. We were so far out of town that the bushes hadn't caught a single newspaper page or burger wrapper in their branches.

Anyone who wanted this place could have it as far as I was concerned. I would have been happy if they lined up everyone in Mexico along the border and started them off like the Oklahoma land rush and let them stake their claims on the land. All this emptiness gave me the creeps although maybe I was the only person living in the Southwest who held that opinion.

I had grown up in LA, but had left for reasons involving a divorce and some differences between me and a fire captain. I was sick of the city and looking for something a little more adventurous. A friend had told me about a job with a fire department south of Tucson. Go to the country and clear my head, that's what I'd been thinking.

Out here on the edge of rattlesnake and scorpion territory they were glad to take me on. I threw my half of the community property into a U-Haul and moved into a house that I'd rented from a bank. Some real estate developer had thought the desert was a great place to build tract housing. My split-level was one of the few he'd completed before he lost his financing. I think I had the Grand Canyon model.

At first, it had been great to breathe fresh air and to see the Milky Way arc overhead. I had driven to the national and state parks and viewed the pueblos. I had admired sunsets over the cacti. But now I'd spent a year in the desert and I was ready to head back to the city where I wouldn't have to eat in rundown diners or chase coyotes away from my garage door.

I also didn't like hearing all the racist crap people were putting out about the "illegals." As far as the locals were concerned everyone coming over the border was a raping, murdering monster. They seemed to think that some sort of invasion was occurring. I sure wasn't going to tell anyone my grandmother's maiden name was Rodriquez.

While the other men continued their discussion, I walked over to Ames to see if I could get him to release me so I didn't have to hang around. None of the people we'd found needed any help from me, that was for sure.

Ames was standing beside his car talking into a radio handset with his back to me. As I walked toward him, I noticed that the bug we'd seen before was fixed on his khaki shirt just below his shoulders.

I ran toward the Ames shouting, "Hey, get away from there" and clapping my hands. As he turned toward me with a look of annoyance the bug flew off. "What's the matter with you?" he asked, "Didn't you see I was calling in my report?"

"That bug was on your back," I told him. "Didn't you feel him sitting there?" Ames said he hadn't felt a thing.

I asked Ames to take off his shirt. I checked his back and found a red welt that I washed with antiseptic. "I can't do anything else for you here, but, if it gets any worse, have your doctor check it out."

The other men had gathered around Ames while I was treating him. Dawson crowed, "I knew that bastard would take a bite out of someone. Now do you see why I took a swing at it?"

Ames didn't have a good come-back to that.

After work I met Sarah for dinner at a Denny's in the suburbs of Tucson. Sarah was "separated but not divorced" and I was "divorced but not looking for a serious commitment." I had met Sarah at a fundraiser for one of the firemen I worked with. His daughter had been diagnosed with leukemia and his friends were trying to help him cover her medical costs.

Sarah was there because one of her boys was in the same class as the sick girl. Neither of us had gone expecting to meet anyone, but we had ended up sharing a pitcher of beer and making conversation about my divorce and her separation and how things you expected to last forever could change overnight. There weren't many potential partners to choose from down there, so if you found someone you were attracted to things could move pretty fast.

For the last three months or so we had hooked up whenever Sarah could find a baby-sitter for her two boys. We'd grab dinner or a movie and she'd come back to my house for an hour or two. She said she couldn't stay over because her children expected her home, although maybe she didn't want to stay over because neither of us was really ready for that sort of relationship yet.

In our round of "tell me how your day was" my story about finding the remains of eight men in the desert trumped Sarah's story about one of her third graders cutting a perfect circle out of construction paper.

"How awful," she exclaimed. "I'd hate to die so far away from home. I hope they'll be able to find their families." I told her that I wasn't sure if they had carried much in the way of personal information because they probably didn't want to have anything to show that they were in the country illegally.

After we had contemplated the horror of the men's deaths for a few minutes I started talking about the bug I'd seen. "You grew up here," I said. "Have you ever come across anything like that?"

"It doesn't sound like anything I've had any experience with," she admitted, but we went down the list of suspects anyway. Cicadas were big, but they didn't bite. Robber flies would bite, but they weren't that big. Scorpions and spiders would bite, but they didn't fly.

"If you run into it again," Sarah said, "try to catch it. My kids would love to see something like that. It would be a great way to start my section on biology."

"Don't you already have enough to tell them about to give them nightmares? Doesn't everything around here bite or sting?" I was making a joke, but she took it seriously.

"People grow up pretty tough in the desert. Sometimes I have to remind my kids that there are times when they should be scared. One recess last year, I had to stop some of my students from poking at a rattlesnake they'd found. They didn't seem to be concerned at all about whether it would strike."

"All I know is that I'm a lot more nervous going outside here than I ever was in LA."

Sarah smiled and put her hand across mine. "Oh, Stu, you're such a scaredy cat. I thought you were a big strong fireman who didn't fear running into a burning building to save women and children. But don't you worry. I'll make sure you get safely to bed tonight."

I laughed. "Thanks. I hope you won't mind me keeping the lights on since I'm scared of the dark."

"Oh, I won't mind. In fact, I insist on it."

I was on duty for the next week living in the firehouse and watching football on TV in the lounge with the other guys. We only had a few call outs and nothing serious, but I always felt some tightness in my stomach while I waited for the next fire to start.

I was enjoying having some down time with nothing in particular to do, so I wasn't happy when the Fire Chief rang my cell phone. Because I was always "on call" I had to pick it up.

For once the Chief seemed hesitant. "You know Deputy Ames, don't you?" the Chief asked. "He was with you last week when you found the border jumpers."

"Yeah," I said. "What's up?"

"Well, the Sheriff just called me. He thinks that Ames has … well, had some sort of nervous breakdown. He says Ames and his family have boarded themselves in Ames' house and are refusing to come out. He's getting ready to smash the door down and he wants someone there who can check Ames' family out."

I got Ames' address from the Chief and started dressing.

Ames lived in a farm house off a dirt road. Five or six men in uniform were standing behind a line of police cars parked about a hundred feet from the front porch. The Sherriff stood in front of them using a bullhorn to try to talk Ames into coming out of the house and surrendering.

As I pulled up, I could hear the Sheriff shouting, "Goddamit Ames, you're a damn fine deputy. Why don't you stop this crap and come out and talk?" One of the other deputies touched the Sheriff on the shoulder and whispered to him, "Ames is very religious guy, boss. He doesn't like profanity."

The Sheriff gave the deputy a look of annoyance. He paused for a few seconds before he raised the bullhorn again and bellowed "Ames, pride and stubbornness are offenses in the eyes of the Lord. I don't know what's happening in your life, but if you step outside we'll all pray together for guidance."

I approached Steve Burroughs, one of the deputies I knew pretty well, and asked what he had heard about what was going on. He told me that Ames had been acting strangely for the past few days. He'd started talking to everyone about the signs of the coming Apocalypse. When he was on duty he'd try to read parts of the bible out loud to the other men.

Yesterday, he didn't come into work. This morning one of his wife's friends had called the Sherriff's office to say that she'd stopped by Ames' house and had found the front door locked and boards nailed across the windows. After she'd knocked she'd heard Ames' wife shouting for help and saying that Ames had "gone crazy."

I said that Ames had seemed perfectly rational when I had seen him the week before. Burroughs shrugged and told me that they'd know pretty soon what was going on. The Sheriff had told his men to break the front door down.

A couple of the deputies pointed rifles at the house while four men went forward with a battering ram. They climbed the steps to the porch and swung the ram against the door which went down with the second blow. I saw the deputies race inside with their guns drawn.

About two minutes went by before they came spilling out of the house covering their heads with their hands. They were followed by a swarm of orange and yellow bugs that shot back and forth over the police cars for a moment before vanishing into the sky. They were almost the size of bats, but I knew what they were. They were bugs like the one I'd seen in the desert.

I ran forward to where men had taken cover and asked if they were hurt. They all said they were okay, but I could see that they were shaken. One of them said, "There's nothing left inside but bones." I had them take their shirts off. They all had two or three red welts on their bodies.

While I tended to the men who had been inside the house the Sheriff and the rest of the deputies peered through the empty door frame. The Sherriff called down to the men on the ground, "What did you see in there, boys? Did you see Ames or anybody from his family?"

A deputy answered back, "Somebody's in there, but you can't tell who it is by looking at him."

As I put antiseptic on their wounds, the men told me what they had found in the house. When they'd noticed a brown stain that ran out from under a bathroom door on the first floor they'd kicked door down. Inside were the skeletons of Ames and his wife and children. It appeared that they had locked themselves in the bathroom and died there. Ames had his service revolver with him.

While they were looking at the bodies someone had noticed a big bug sitting on the shoulder of one of the other deputies. First there had been one, then others had shown up. When they started to swarm the deputies had retreated through the house and run outside. None of them had realized they were bitten until I insisted on checking them out.

Even though the men all insisted that they were fine, I told the Sheriff that he should have someone take the men to the ER. I told the

Sheriff that I didn't know what had injured the men and I didn't know if there was any risk of infection.

The Sheriff said that he was short-handed and didn't want to release anyone from duty unless he was really sick. He added, "I hope that you aren't suggesting that any of my boys need grief-counseling or anything like that." I told the Sheriff I knew his men were tough, but if anybody showed any symptoms like running a fever he should get that man to the hospital fast.

When I got home I went through the house looking for bugs. I found a spider or two, but nothing I considered dangerous.

I spent the night researching flying insects of the world on the internet, but I didn't find my bug. The Japanese Hornet was about the right size and shape, but the coloring was wrong and though it had big jaws they weren't as big as the ones I'd seen. Not that the Japanese Hornet was anything to sneeze at. It had a bite that could melt human flesh and, if you upset it, it would chase you for up to three miles. It made me realize that not everything bad in the world lived in the Arizona desert.

As I was doing my research I came across a couple of websites that made me even more anxious than I had been that afternoon. I read about a parasitic wasp that lays eggs on a spider. The larva hatch and inject some substance into the spider's blood that makes it a sort of zombie. The spider weaves itself into a cocoon where the larva can finish it off in peace.

There's a fungus that infects the brains of ants so they hang themselves upside down from leaves and let the fungi grow through their bodies. There's a worm that infects grasshoppers and makes them commit suicide by jumping into water where the worms can escape and reproduce.

Sure, you say, but that's just worms and insects. Parasite couldn't do something like that to a mammal. Well, how about *Toxoplasma gandii*? It infects cats, but it does so by first infecting rats. When it gets inside a rat it excretes chemicals that cause the rat to lose its instinctual fear of cats. The infected rat goes out and cozies up to a cat and the cat makes the rat into an easy dinner. Then the parasite is inside the cat where it wanted to be all along.

This was crazy stuff, of course. No one said that there was any parasite that infected humans and gave them psychotic episodes, but after what I'd seen, I was wondering if something new had come up from Mexico with the illegals we'd found in the desert.

I knew there wasn't much point in telling officialdom about my suspicions. I didn't know if they'd laugh when I told them about zombie spiders, but I was pretty sure that they'd take away my job and maybe put me under observation.

Just keep a clear head, I told myself, just wait and see what happens next. However, while I was telling myself to stay alert I was going through a pint of Jack. I ended up sleeping on the floor next to the computer.

When I woke up the next morning I found, first, that I had a headache and, second, that Sarah had called me and left a message on my answering machine. Sarah wanted to see me. She sounded sort of desperate.

I called her back on her cell phone although I knew that she would be at school. She answered, but before I could even say "hello," she told me to meet her at the Denny's at 7:00 that night and as soon as I had agreed to be there she said she had to get back to her class. She whispered she'd tell me what was going on when she saw me and hung up.

When I walked into the restaurant a few minutes after 7:00 I found that Sarah had taken a seat at one of the tables and was polishing off her first margarita. I thought she looked a bit frazzled.

There wasn't any small talk. Sarah started off her part of the conversation in a rush. Her husband, Lewis, had filed divorce papers and had asked for primary custody of the children. "My lawyer says he won't get it," she said, "but he also told me that I've got to be careful, that Lewis will be looking for any proof that I'm not entirely fit to be the custodial parent. He said I should avoid any sort of relationship that might reflect badly on my reputation."

I didn't like where this was going. "So I'm the sort of relationship that might reflect badly on your reputation."

"Look, Stu, I'm ... well, fond of you, but you've only been here for a year and we both know that you're thinking of leaving. You haven't spent any time with my children and I'm sure you're not itching to take on the role of father figure. My relationship with you is essentially going out to bars and then going back to your house to screw. This is a pretty conservative community. I don't think that is the sort of relationship that is going to impress a family court judge."

I didn't know what to say. I was thinking through my options when Sarah drained her glass and stood up. "Listen, Stu, I'm not pressuring you to make our relationship a more permanent thing. I'm not looking for another husband. I just wanted to tell you in person that I was ending things between us. I won't do anything that might cost me my children. I'm sorry, but that's just the way it is."

She mumbled, "I'm sorry" again and threw a twenty dollar bill on the table. I guess that was to pay for her drink. I was about to say something like *I don't come that cheap* when she walked past me and went out the swinging doors of the restaurant.

Five minutes after she left I remembered that I had wanted to tell her about the bugs. I had wanted to warn her. I thought about trying to reach her on her cell phone, but I figured that she wasn't going to answer any of my calls.

The waiter came over while I fretted. I ordered Jack straight up and a cheeseburger. I could feel myself veering between extremes. I felt like Sarah was acting like a goddam fool, but I also wanted to run out and rescue her.

I had finished my drink by the time the waiter brought the cheeseburger to my table. I ordered another Jack and drank it while I ate. By the end of the meal all I had decided was that I had to be very careful driving home if I didn't want to lose my license.

I was on duty the next day. There were four of us at the firehouse. We all got along pretty well. Bobby cooked for us and he was great at making Italian dishes. Ed was always trying to get us to play poker, but he liked to play for higher stakes than the rest of felt comfortable with. Dupree was sort of quiet, but every once in a while he would make some comment that got us all laughing.

During the day, while we washed the fire engine or cleaned the other equipment we kept the radio on. The other guys liked listening to the morning talk show. People called in with all sorts of crazy political opinions. The trend was pretty conservative, so I usually found something to do at the other end of the station while it was on.

I was washing dishes when Ed called up to me, "Stu, you've got to come hear this. This guy is really over the top." I wiped my hands and went downstairs to listen.

The guy who had called in was obsessed with "the greys." He said that the greys had landed at Roswell and that they were being held at Area 51. Now other greys were here and they were carrying people away to some lab they had built in one of the National Forests. He spoke in a low intense voice with a sort of Southern drawl.

The host was egging the guy on. Tell us about the spaceships, he'd say. Tell us about the shadows. The caller was sounding more and more frantic. They're everywhere, he said. They hide in the shadows and zap you with their ray guns which take away your free will.

"Tell us about the anal probing," the host said.

After about a half hour, you could hear the guy completely lose it. He shouted, "You can make all the jokes you want, but I've seen them. I know they're real. I've got a shotgun and I've got a fallout shelter in my basement. I'm going to stay in there until they drag me out and you ought to do the same." He finished with some comment that got blipped and then he slammed the phone down.

Ed and Bobby thought this was hilarious. They were laughing and pretending to shoot each other with ray guns. Dupree walked away, but I sat down on one of the benches.

"What's the matter?" Ed asked. "You look worried. Do think that we've got greys hiding in the fire station?" I shook my head. What I was thinking about was the caller's voice. He had sounded just like one of the Deputies I had treated at the Ames house.

That night Dupree seemed more subdued than usual. He sat watching TV while the rest of us ate the meatballs Bobby had made and played cards. I asked Ed what was going on with Dupree and he told me that Dupree had seemed upset about the government. Ed didn't know what had set him off.

After a while I went over to the couch and sat next to Dupree. I asked him if anything was going on. I could see sweat on his forehead. He shook his head. "No," he said, "nothing in particular. Just that the country's going downhill, that's all. It used to be great, but now it's got all these taxmen and the FBI and the CIA snooping around and bugging people's telephones."

I said something noncommittal and went back to the card game. I told the guys that I thought that something was seriously wrong with Dupree and maybe we should try to get him some medical care. They said I was overreacting. "He's just in a bad mood," Bobby insisted. "He's been complaining that his belly is acting up. He'll be fine tomorrow."

I tried to keep an eye on Dupree, but about midnight he went downstairs. I turned in for the night after that and surprised myself by almost immediately falling asleep. When I woke up at 6:00 the next morning I noticed that Dupree had never come back to his cot.

I got my shoes on and went downstairs. I didn't see him, but when I checked the door to the downstairs restroom I found that it was locked. I knocked, but there was no response although I thought that I could hear some sort of movement behind the door.

I called Bobby and Ed to come down and bring the key with them. The door to the restroom locks from the inside, but you can open it with a key. We have to keep it locked because a couple of homeless guys have snuck in when we had the garage doors open and have made a mess in there.

Ed knocked and then turned the key. We peered in and almost immediately backtracked. Ed slammed the door shut and locked it again. Bobby ran to the back wall and retched. "Jesus Christ," Ed sputtered. "Did you see that?"

We'd all seen Dupree's body lying on the rest room floor. His face was covered with white maggots the size of a man's fist. Things were moving under Dupree's clothes so it seemed like the maggots were working over the rest of his body, too.

Ed pulled out his cell phone and called 911. No one answered. Ed looked at me. "There's always supposed to be someone at that number," he said. "What the hell is going on here? Where the hell did those frigging maggots come from?"

I told Ed that I thought that Dupree might have brought them in himself even though he didn't know it. Bobby straightened up and wiped his mouth. "What exactly are you saying, Stu? Do you know something about this?" He sounded more than a little shaky.

I told them about the men in the desert and tried to explain what I thought was happening. I said that the bugs were infecting people with parasites and that when you got infected you ended up isolating yourself until the parasites came bursting out of you and fed on your body. I'm sure this sounded ridiculous, but after seeing those maggots eating Dupree everyone was ready to accept my story.

"So where's the Sheriff?" Bobby asked. I said that I thought most of the police had been infected when they broke into Ames' place. Maybe the rest of them were protecting their families or trying to get the hell out of town.

Bobby and Ed had families, too. Ed said it first, "I've got to get home." Bobby was already headed out the door. They were both good fire fighters, but right then they didn't care whether the station was manned or not. As Ed got in his car, he shouted that he'd give me a call once he checked things out at home.

I found some dish towels upstairs in the kitchen and stuffed them under the door to the bathroom. I figured that would keep the maggots from getting out. I wasn't going to get a fire axe and go *mano a maggato*. I'd seen how easily there were taking the flesh off Dupree.

My guess was that the maggots were only an intermediate stage. I wasn't sure how long it would take, but I was positive that they'd turn into bugs once they'd finished their meal. There was an air conditioning vent in the bathroom. It was probably too small to let them get into the rest of the fire station, but I didn't want to take that chance.

I decided that my best bet was to make a run for Tucson. They had hospitals and labs there. They had a SWAT team and they could call in the military. Somebody there would be able to figure out what to do about the bugs.

But first I was going to call Sarah. I could swing by her house on my way out of town and pick up her and her children. At least, I could give her a warning. If she was still worried about being seen with me she could drive to Tucson herself.

I wasn't positive that Sarah would answer my call, but she picked up after the third ring. She seemed frantic. "Oh, Stu," she exclaimed, "you've got to help me. They're here. They're all over the front yard."

"Don't let the bugs in," I shouted back. "Keep your doors and...."

Sarah interrupted. "Bugs? What the hell do bugs have to do with it? It's the men that I'm talking about. They're spying on me. My husband must have hired them. Maybe they're detectives, or black ops. They're hiding outside. They're just waiting for me to come out."

She must have turned away for a moment. I could hear her sobbing. Then she returned to the phone and shouted, "They're trying to take my kids away. But I won't let them. I'm going take them into the crawlspace. They'll never find us."

"No! Don't try to hide anywhere. Stay there. I'll come pick you up."

I heard another voice. It was a child saying, "Mommy, why can't I go outside?"

The line went dead. I was in my car in a second. I knew where Sarah lived. I'd dropped her off one day when she had to take her car into the garage for repairs. I was thinking that, if I could get her to a hospital, they could do something before… well, I didn't want to think about what might happen.

Two blocks from the fire station, I stopped for a man crossing the street. When he halted and turned toward me I realized that he was carrying a shotgun. I lifted my foot from the brake and spurted forward, but he fired both barrels into the rear of my car. I scooted over the sidewalk and into the plate glass window of a hardware store. I hit my head on the steering wheel and lost consciousness.

I don't know how much time passed before I pulled myself out of the car. I crawled over to the wall and propped myself up against a shelf holding small appliances. Nothing was broken, so far as I could tell, but I had a ringing in my head.

When I could stand I staggered over to the hole I'd made in the store's façade and looked down the street. I was hoping that the guy with the shotgun wouldn't bother to come over and finish me off. He was gone, but I could see a bug resting on the roof of the bus stop across the street.

I was exposed here. I had to find some shelter. All I could think of was to get back to the fire station. My body was telling me that I needed to rest. Instead I set off at a lope down the street and didn't stop until I was upstairs in the firemen's living quarters where I threw myself across our sofa and put my hands over my eyes. I knew that I probably had a concussion and that the last thing that I should do was fall asleep, but before I could think about it I was out.

When I came to, the station was dark. I climbed to my feet and felt along the wall for the light switch. A day before, I wouldn't have even considered the possibility that the power would have been off. Now when I flipped on the lights it seemed like a miracle had occurred.

I took a quick look through the upstairs and didn't see any bugs. I eased myself downstairs and searched the garage. It seemed clean although I could hear buzzing behind the door to the bathroom.

I needed two things before I went out on the streets again. First, I went to the locker where we kept our HAZMAT suits. The Chief had talked the county into purchasing them after the last anthrax scare. I zipped myself in, checked the face plate and made sure I could breathe. Then, I went looking for the keys to the pumper.

I wasn't certified to drive the pumper, but right now who cared? I was pretty sure that no one was going to take this baby down with a shotgun. After I started the engine I used the electric opener to raise the garage door. I turned on the siren and the flashers in the hope that it would scare away the bugs or tell people to get out of my way and, besides, why not?

The streets were empty as I drove to Sarah's house. I parked in her driveway with the headlights shining on her front door. I slammed my fist against her front door and shouted, "Sarah, are you okay."

When no one came to the door I started around the side to check the back way in. As I passed her front window I notice that the curtains had moved. I shouted, "Sarah," again and moved as close to the window as I could without ripping my suit in the shrubbery. I could see bugs crawling up and down inside on the glass.

I went back to the pumper and turned off the siren and the lights. There wasn't so much as a porch light left on in the neighborhood. I sat in the darkness and thought about Sarah and thought about what the hell I would do now. After a few minutes, I started the engine, turned on the headlights and drove through the silent town to my house out on the edge of the desert.

I kept the HAZMAT suit on as I worked my way through every room in my house. When I was sure that no bugs had gotten in I got out of the suit and took a hot shower. I stayed in the shower for at least fifteen minutes. The shower had fogged the mirror, so I cleaned it one of towels I kept by the sink. I turned around in the front of the mirror and found the red welt on my right side just under my shoulder.

104

I sat down at my desk and typed this story on my computer. I tried to send it out by email, but the wireless service wasn't working, so I'm saving it under the file name "Fear" in case anyone comes looking for it.

When I first got here and I started sight-seeing I heard about the Anazasi, the ancient ones, who lived in the Southwest. The guides said that their culture disappeared about a thousand years ago. Some said they left because the place stopped getting a regular rainfall. Some said they migrated and started their culture elsewhere. I have to wonder whether the bugs came up from the South and wiped them out. Maybe someone else will be around to figure that one out.

My head is telling me that the desert is full of danger. Snakes and scorpions and packs of coyotes and the bugs, too, are out there waiting for me. I can hear them as they sniff and fly, crawl and slither around my house. I can feel my heart beating faster as I contemplate their terrors and all I want to do is hide.

But I'm going to force myself to go outside. I'm going to climb into the front seat of the pumper and drive to Tucson or whatever civilized place is left and get help. Maybe, they can do something about this parasite I've got. Even if they can't, they'll at least know that I'm telling them the truth when they see my belly rip open and something disgusting climb out. I'd rather die there than here.

All I've got to do is go outside and get into that pumper and drive. That's all I've got to do. Just move.